2/3/89

WINNER TAKES ALL

Jonathan and Trish were strolling across the lawn together in the moonlight. Trish's breath caught in her throat.

"Hello," he said slowly, taking hold of her hand.

"Hello," she responded shyly, giving his hand a slight squeeze. He returned the pressure, and she felt as if there was a rocket about to be launched in her chest. Trish knew that she couldn't be luckier; she was with the sweetest boy she had ever met.

They started down the narrow stairs to the dock side by side, her hip brushing against his. She felt so light-headed that, even though these were the same stairs she had climbed at least a million times before, her feet moved awkwardly, as uncertain of themselves as the rest of her was.

"I've been waiting to talk to you all evening," Jonathan said.

Her heart started beating even faster.

Bantam Sweet Dreams Romances
Ask your bookseller for the books you have missed

Winner Takes All

Laurie Lykken

BANTAM BOOKS
TORONTO · NEW YORK · LONDON · SYDNEY · AUCKLAND

RL 6, IL age 11 and up

WINNER TAKES ALL
A Bantam Book/July 1988

*Sweet Dreams and its associated logo are registered trademarks of
Bantam Books, Inc. Registered in U.S. Patent and Trademark Office
and elsewhere.*

Cover photo by Pat Hill.

ISBN 0-553-26790-6

Published simultaneously in the United States and Canada

*Bantam Books are published by Bantam Books, Inc. Its trademark,
consisting of the words "Bantam Books" and the portrayal of
a rooster, is Registered in U.S. Patent and Trademark Office
and in other countries. Marca Registrada. Bantam Books, Inc.,
666 Fifth Avenue, New York, New York 10103.*

Printed and bound in Great Britain by
Cox & Wyman Ltd., Reading

Winner Takes All

Chapter One

"It's awfully windy," Mary said, her small, up-turned nose pressed against the glass of the Everetts' kitchen window.

Peering over the dark curls that topped her best friend's head, Trish had to agree. Sand Lake, one of the largest lakes in Minnesota, did look turbulent, but saying so might frighten Mary. Still, if they didn't take the boat out for a sail that day, they never would. If Trish gave in to the nervous feeling that gripped her insides at the thought of pleasure sailing, how would she ever have the courage to race?

Mary straightened up and turned around. "Maybe Clark would go out on the lake with us."

The last thing Trish wanted was to go running to her brother at the first sign of a stiff wind. It was just what Clark was waiting for, just what he expected her to do. Clark didn't want her to skip the boat at all—even though he was going away for most of the summer. He had even tried to talk their parents out of letting Trish have her chance.

She shook her head. "We can handle it without Clark," Trish replied, wishing she felt as certain of that as she had back in March when the lake had still been covered with ice and snow. "I'll race the boat!" she remembered declaring the night Clark had announced his plans to spend eight weeks in Maine at a sailing camp. At that time she believed she could do it.

"Come on," Trish said, taking hold of her best friend's hand. "Let's go. Standing here worrying isn't getting us anywhere."

"Well, let's hope it's safe," Mary countered, allowing herself to be led in the direction of the back door.

The two friends were a study in contrasts. While Trish was tall and thin, Mary was short and round. Trish had shoulder-length, straight blond hair, wispy bangs, and blue eyes. Mary had dark hair that was short and curly, and her eyes were brown.

When they reached the bottom of the white-washed steps, Trish ducked into the boat house for the sails. Coming out, she found Mary stretched out on her stomach on the dock reaching for the water.

"Oooh!" Mary wailed, pulling her hand away as if she'd just touched fire. "I thought you said this lake had thawed." She gave Trish a dirty look.

"It was your idea to stick your hand in it, silly, not mine," Trish said, laughing, as she stepped over her. "How did you expect lake water to feel at the end of May?" Because it was so large, Sand Lake was slower to warm than the other lakes in the Minneapolis area.

"Maybe we should forget sailing today," Mary suggested, getting to her feet. "Why don't we wait until the water warms up a bit?"

"If we're going to be ready to race in a couple of weeks, we've got to practice," Trish reminded her. "Besides," she added, "we're going sailing—not swimming."

"I guess you're right," Mary conceded grudgingly.

Trish crossed her fingers behind her back. "Of course I'm right."

The brisk, spring wind was sending little ripples every which way across the surface of the lake, while the poplars along the shore made a swishing noise as they swayed. "Let's get that boat rigged," Trish said, feeling even less confident than she had up at the house.

But Mary didn't seem to notice. "OK. Tell me what to do, skipper, and I'll do it," she said.

Leaning over, Trish pulled the boat closer to the dock. Taking out two yellow life jackets, she said, "We'd better put these on." Mary's round, pixielike face clouded over.

"Why do I need this? You're not trying to tell me something, are you? We never wore life jackets when we went sailing before."

"We never raced together before, either. Up until now, we've just fooled around. We have to wear life jackets during a race, and we need to get used to moving around in them, OK?" Mary slipped the life jacket on, and Trish waved her onto the boat.

Once Mary was on board, Trish hopped on the boat herself and began pointing out the parts of the boat to her friend. Although Mary had been sailing before, it was only for fun; she'd never been in a race.

Deciding she could go into the particulars later, Trish stuck to the basics. She didn't want to overwhelm Mary with a lot of sailing jargon—it was bad enough that it was so windy their first time out. Trish knew how hard it was to find a willing, regular crew, and she didn't want to risk losing Mary.

Trish had had plenty of experience as a crew member. As a skipper, however, she had nearly none. Trish had skipped the boat three times in Clark's place, and each race had been a disaster in its own way! But she suspected it was probably because she'd gotten one of Clark's standby's for a crew every time, and it was always a different, impatient boy.

"Let's rig the boat," Trish said to Mary, trying to forget those experiences. But as they threaded the large mainsail along the boom of the sixteen-foot, flat-bottomed sailboat, Trish wondered if Mary would have been as willing to commit herself to crew all summer if she had crewed for

Trish during her previous disasters. Trish doubted it, even though Mary was her best friend.

This year would be different, though. Trish was fifteen, and although she was only one year older, she felt she could handle the pressures of racing now. Reaching into the pocket of her shorts, she took out an elastic band and pulled her blond hair back into a ponytail so it wouldn't keep blowing in her eyes.

"And next," she told Mary, "you hoist the jib. OK?"

Mary scowled. "I think so—if you remind me what the jib is."

Trish pointed to the smaller of the two sails crumpled on the bow of the boat. "It's that little sail over there."

Reaching toward the tangle of lines running down the mast, Mary paused again. "Which rope was it?"

"Line," Trish reminded her.

"Huh?" Mary's dark brows came together in confusion.

"Line," Trish repeated patiently. "On a boat, you call the ropes lines." Trish pulled one of the lines out of the tangled mess and handed it to Mary.

"This is a special line called a halyard, which is used to raise and lower a sail. This is the jib halyard. There's also a halyard for the mainsail."

"Will I ever learn all this?" Mary wailed. She looked directly at Trish. "Maybe you'd be better off if someone else crewed. You know, someone with more experience."

Who? Trish asked herself silently. Aloud, she said, "You'll learn. We're going to have fun."

Soon they had the sails up and were gliding across the lake. The wind was brisk but warm, and Trish felt herself relax. After all, she had been sailing ever since she could sit up, and she had been racing since she was nine. She felt foolish for having had any doubts about her own abilities. Everything was going to be fine, despite Clark's prediction that she'd sink the boat.

Of course Clark was the champion of the fleet, and Trish had never really had a chance before this to do much more than be in his crew. They were also very close in age. With only eleven months separating them, Trish was forced to wait for him to outgrow certain things before she got her own chance.

Clark did lead the way for her. And because they looked so much alike, people always knew Trish was his sister. Not only did they have the same blond hair and blue eyes, they were also about the same height and had the same slender build as well. In fact, they were often mistaken for twins.

The biggest difference between them was on the inside. Clark was the dashing, adventurous one, while Trish was—what? She had lived in Clark's shadow for so long that she wasn't sure, but she longed to find out. Three disastrous races didn't make Trish an all-time loser, no matter what Clark seemed to think—or did they?

Trish looked across the cockpit at Mary, and seeing her friend's round face and glowing cheeks made her remember some of the good feelings she had had back in March when she demanded to be given the opportunity to skip the boat while Clark was away. Her parents had had enough faith in her to say yes.

Suddenly she felt an extra tug on both the mainsheet and the tiller as a very strong gust of wind slammed into the sail. Trish tightened her grip on the line and began paying more attention to the movement of the wind across the water. It wasn't the time to daydream.

The gust passed, but she noticed that the overall wind had picked up. She felt a slight twinge in her left arm. For the first time it occurred to Trish that she might not be physically strong enough to skip the boat for an entire race during a heavy wind. But she told herself that that was why she was out practicing, to learn things while she still had the time to do something about it.

"Coming about," she called, getting ready to head back to the dock. She didn't want to get any farther out on the lake, since she was beginning to tire. Besides, it would be good to call an end to their sailing while Mary was still having fun.

Mary smiled at her. "This is great!" she said, enthusiastically.

"You'd better duck," Trish warned. "I'm going to come about, and that boom is going to whip across the boat."

Mary dipped effortlessly under the sail.

"That was great. You need to keep your movements smooth so you don't rock the boat." As she complimented Mary, Trish found herself wishing she had Mary's short, compact body instead of her own long, lanky one. Everything Mary did looked graceful. No wonder she had the cutest boyfriend in the whole school while Trish had no steady boyfriend at all. In fact, she could still count the number of dates she had had on the fingers of one hand.

"I love this. Why haven't we ever gone out in a wind like this before?" Mary asked. Clearly, her earlier fear had changed into exhilaration.

Glad that everything was working out so well, Trish shrugged, even though she knew perfectly well why she had never done much sailing in strong winds. Clark had always made it clear that *Lucky Lady* was his boat. Either he was out sailing himself or he was telling Trish she'd never be able to handle the boat without him. But now, for at least eight weeks, *Lucky Lady* belonged to Trish!

The wind blew up again, and Trish felt another twinge of pain. This time it was across the muscles of her back. She wished the dock were closer! Deciding the fastest way in would be a starboard beat, Trish pulled the mainsail in as tight as she could and pointed the bow of the boat upwind.

"Pull in the jib, and on the way in to the dock, I'll show you how to hike out," Trish said, kicking at the thick, nylon straps bolted to the wooden frame of the cockpit. She slipped her ankles into the straps, and Mary followed her lead. Trish soon found, though, that holding the tiller prevented her from leaning her own weight very far out over the edge of the boat.

"Lean out farther!" she yelled to Mary, who was copying Trish too closely. They needed more weight out over the water in order to level the boat. If they rode up any higher, the rudder might leave the water altogether, and Trish would lose control of *Lucky Lady*.

She was about to remedy the situation by letting the sails out a little when the boat suddenly lurched upward. It was as if a huge hand had slipped beneath the boat. In a split second, they went over. Both Mary and Trish were tossed into the icy, late May water.

"Are you all right?" Trish asked when Mary finally surfaced. Mary looked frightened, but she managed to nod. "Grab onto the boat and don't let go," Trish ordered.

Trish was thankful that she had insisted they both wear life jackets. Besides giving them buoyancy, the jackets would help keep them warm. Trish had had plenty of experience tipping over in cold water, but she had never had to get the boat upright by herself. There was Mary, of course, but Mary had no experience tipping over at all.

9

"We better pull the sail down before it fills up with water and tips the boat completely upside down," she told Mary in a completely calm voice that seemed to come from somewhere outside her body.

"Can't we just flip this thing back up?" Mary's voice rattled with the cold.

Trish nodded. "Yes, but first we've got to pull the sail down." She looked at Mary and added, "You stay put, I'll get the sail down myself."

She began swimming around the boat uncleating the lines and pulling at the Dacron mainsail, pausing frequently to look toward the shore for some sign that help was on its way. Her joints were already throbbing from the cold. Even Clark, she told herself, would be a welcome sight. And it was just possible that he had been watching her every move from the house and had seen them go over. It was something he'd do, especially in his present state over her skipping the boat.

"Still there?" Trish asked, pulling herself back to where she had left Mary.

Mary nodded. "Just tell me what to do," she said in short gasps. "And I'll do it."

Trish looked toward shore again, but there was no one in sight.

"Let's try to right her. If you should lose hold of the boat," Trish cautioned Mary, "don't take your life jacket off, no matter what, OK?" She didn't add that she might drown without the jacket, although the look on Mary's face told Trish that Mary knew that already.

They maneuvered themselves around the boat, and Trish tugged the heavy metal sideboard that had come out of its sheath and was now above the water on the high side of the boat. This was not an easy task. Usually, the weight of a board made it drop once its line was loosened. But, with *Lady* on her side, there was no weight to make the high board drop, so it had to be lowered manually. The low board was down, but, being underwater, it was of no help.

With two sideboards, one board was always tucked away while the other board was lowered. Each time they came about, the boards had to be switched so that the leeward board was down and the windward board was up. Alternating this way, the two boards acted as if they were keels for *Lady*'s flat bottom. Without either board down, *Lucky Lady* would slide sideways across the water; with both of them down, the boat would become unsteerable.

Trish climbed onto the flat, metal-gray surface of the board, and Mary followed her lead. Being out of the water was even colder than being in the water, and Trish noticed that her best friend's lips were turning blue.

"Now we bounce," Trish told Mary. "That'll warm us up." She tried to smile, but only half her mouth would turn up. Trish knew her own lips were undoubtedly blue from cold, too.

They began bouncing on the high board. For a moment it looked as if they'd be able to do it. Then Mary slipped, and fell back into the lake.

Trish felt beaten. Clark was right—she had no business going out on the lake. Just as Trish felt a tear of hopelessness trickle warmly down her cheek, she heard the sound of a motorboat coming closer and closer.

"We're saved!" Trish cried.

Expecting to see Clark or possibly her father racing toward them, she turned toward the sound with relief. But the boat coming rapidly in their direction wasn't the Everetts' red outboard. Instead it was a large, blue cruiser, the kind of boat used for waterskiing.

"Who's that?" Trish wondered out loud.

"Who cares!" Mary shot back. "I love them, whoever they are." Pulling herself onto the high side of the boat, Mary sat down next to Trish.

When the motorboat finally reached them, Trish didn't recognize either the boat or the boy driving it. But Mary was right, this was no time to worry about such things.

"Hey, there," the boy called over the roar of his idling engine, "need some help getting your boat righted?"

"Y-y-yes," Trish managed to sputter.

Mary gave her a light poke with her elbow. "Speak louder," she hissed, without taking her eyes off the rescuer.

"Yes!" Trish yelled with more force.

"Smile," Mary ordered.

Trish turned to see if Mary had gone into shock, but, aside from being wet and obviously cold, she seemed to be in full possession of herself. Trish was still examining Mary when Mary smiled at her.

"Don't look so cross," Mary commanded through her smile. She motioned toward the speedboat with her head. "Try to look a little friendlier."

Trish looked at their rescuer again. She could see he was their age or possibly a little older. Was Mary actually suggesting that she flirt with him right in the middle of being rescued? She peered back at Mary and knew by the silly smirk on her face that Mary most certainly was!

"Get your boom out of the water," the boy directed. "Even with your sail down it's still catching water." He stood as he gestured, and Trish noted that he was tall and well-built. "Cleat the mainsheet to the deck," he went on, a calm authority to his voice that felt soothing. "That'll hold the boom out of the water. Then get out on that high board, and I'll give your mast a toss." Without waiting for them to move, he maneuvered his boat around to the top of their mast.

"Come on," Mary said, starting to climb out on the sideboard.

Trish grabbed her wrist to stop her. "Your shoes don't have enough traction. You're likely to hurt yourself if you fall off the board again."

Mary nodded thoughtfully. "I'll have to get some boat shoes before we race, won't I?"

Trish wanted to hug her. After all that, Mary was *still* planning on crewing for her. "Oh, Mary—" she started to say.

"Hey," the boy yelled up to them. "I'm ready when you are."

Trish yelled back, "Her shoes are too slippery!"

"Have her hang onto that mainsheet you cleated to the deck to hold the boom out of the water," he responded. "We need both of you out there to get the boat up."

"I'll be OK," Mary insisted when Trish shook her head doubtfully. "I just want to be warm again."

Trish knew how Mary felt because she felt the same way herself. She leaned over the edge of the boat, took hold of the cleated mainsheet, and handed the line to her friend. Mary wrapped it around her waist, and they began bouncing. Together they set the boat in motion. On the count of three, the boy gave the mast a forceful toss. Mary and Trish fell back into the water, but *Lucky Lady* was upright! Dripping, they climbed back aboard the water-filled boat.

Both girls began to shiver. Trish glanced at the soggy sail hanging in wet folds on either side of the boom. It was too wet to do more than flap halfheartedly from it's position a quarter of the way up the mast, even though the wind was as strong, or stronger, than ever. Upon seeing this, the consequences of their accident finally struck Trish. Even if Mary was still willing to be her crew, Trish was not at all certain whether her parents, undoubtedly encouraged by her brother, would still be willing to let her skip *Lucky Lady* during the yacht club races.

"Want a tow back to your dock?" th
asked, gliding up beside them. He watch
they fumbled with the wet sails knee-dee
bilge water. Then he chuckled. "The lake is still
a little cold for swimming, isn't it?"

Trish felt the muscles in her back tighten as
she turned, prepared to tell him off for laughing at their predicament. But when she looked
into his emerald-green eyes, she felt herself melt.
Mary was right. He was very good-looking. Suddenly Trish realized how *she* must look. She
suspected that she resembled a half-drowned
rat. Feeling a few wisps of wet hair clinging to
her cheeks told her that her hastily bound, blond
hair was coming loose.

Despite her shivering body, Trish's cheeks
began to burn. She was so embarrassed that
she realized she had forgotten why she was
irritated.

"You can say that again." Mary laughed. "And,
yes, we'd love a tow." Trish looked over at her
friend and wondered how she could still look so
cute and act so composed when she was so wet
and cold.

"You're a hero, you know," Mary went on.
Then she batted her long, dark eyelashes at
him. Trish felt a sharp poke in her ribs. "Isn't
he, Trish?" Mary demanded pointedly.

Trish bobbed her head up and down, feeling increasingly foolish.

"I guess you *are* lucky that I happened to be
out on my dock when you went over. There

isn't too much activity out here today. You might have had yourselves a long wait. By the way," he added, "my name is Jonathan Stewart."

"This is Trish Everett," Mary said, grabbing Trish's arm and waving it at him, "and my name is Mary."

"Why don't you both ride in the motorboat with me?" Jonathan suggested. "I can tie your boat to the stern of my cruiser."

"I think I should stay with the boat just in case," Trish said.

"In case of what?" Mary asked.

Unable to think of anything, Trish shrugged.

"I'll stay with the boat," Mary announced, giving Trish a push toward the motorboat. "You go with Jonathan. You know the way back to your house better than I do anyway."

Too numb to argue, Trish sloshed through the water-logged cockpit to get the painter, a short line that clipped onto the bow of the boat and was used to secure it to a dock. Now, however, it would be used to connect the two boats during the tow.

Trish climbed into Jonathan's cruiser. She felt ugly, dumb, and totally inept. Part of her hoped she would never see Jonathan Stewart again, even though he was possibly the cutest boy she had ever seen. Or perhaps it was precisely because he *was* one of the cutest boys she had ever seen that she felt so horribly embarrassed.

"Here," he said, taking off his jacket and handing it to Trish. "You can give this to your friend."

Trish took the jacket and crawled across both boats to give it to Mary, who was sitting in the stern holding the tiller. Snuggling into it as though it were mink, Mary smiled and waved at Jonathan who smiled and waved back.

"Am I supposed to try and steer with this thing?" Mary asked, indicating the tiller.

Trish shook her head. "Just hold it steady. Both boards are up. The boat should just swing behind his cruiser. You could really put the tiller in this and ride with us if you want to," Trish told her, raising a little wooden crutch that had slots to hold both the tiller and the boom securely in place.

"I'm fine back here," Mary said. "Besides, my feet feel warm in this water." She indicated the more than three inches of water that filled *Lady*'s cockpit.

"If you're sure," Trish said.

"I'm sure—and I'm cold. Go on back to his boat," Mary urged. "I want to get home."

Trish climbed back to *Lady*'s bow and crossed from her boat to Jonathan's. She saw that he had tied the line to the stern of his cruiser along a rod that would be used to tow water-skiers.

"This is for you," he told Trish as she took the seat behind him. He'd taken off his chocolate-brown chamois shirt and was holding it out to her.

"I can't," she protested, trying not to stare at his tanned, muscular arms, or at the goose-flesh that the cold air had created.

"Of course you can," he insisted, still holding the shirt out to her.

"But you need it," Trish countered. "You're already cold."

"Better we're all a little cold than one of us freezes to death. Go on," he insisted again. "Take it."

Feeling even more awkward and ridiculous than before, Trish took the shirt. She slipped her arms into the soft, brushed cotton sleeves. "Thanks," she mumbled, wishing she could melt into the blue vinyl seat and disappear.

"What's wrong?" he asked, shivering slightly. Trish knew he was colder than he was letting on.

"You're cold," she said, feeling a rush of concern for him.

His boat moved slowly forward, and *Lucky Lady*'s sixteen-foot, waterlogged hull swung slowly around behind it. He shrugged. "A little," he confessed. "But at least I'm dry. I'm sure both of you girls are much colder, as wet as you are. How long were you out there before I showed up?"

Trish thought again of how awful she must look. "Not too long," she answered. But then added, "But long enough."

Jonathan gave her a sympathetic look. "I wish I had something to cover your legs with. I used to have a blanket on the boat, but I took it out last fall and never put it back. I guess the best thing would be to get you home quickly."

At that point, he opened the engine up some more. The noise made any further conversation impossible. Trish had to direct him to her dock with hand motions.

In no time at all, they were at the Everetts'. Trish let the line that held the two boats together go, and *Lady* drifted to the dock. Mary reached out and caught the dock.

Jonathan put his own boat into reverse and then into neutral, coming to a halt alongside the dock farther up, nearer the shore. He crossed the boat and grabbed onto the dock. "Mind if I tie up here for a minute?" he asked.

Trish shook her head. "Of course not." She looked over at Mary, who was trying to tie *Lady* to the dock with the painter. "Excuse me, though. First I'd better help Mary."

As Trish started to step onto the dock, she heard sneakered feet on the wooden steps behind her. Turning, she looked up and saw Clark trotting toward her, looking furious. She expected him to stop when he reached her, but he swept right past her.

Mary, who was still struggling to tie the boat up, looked at him and smiled. He didn't smile back. Instead he snatched the short line from her and tied the boat to the dock himself. Then he turned and stormed back to where Trish was now standing.

"What happened?" he demanded, his hands planted firmly on his hips.

Something inside Trish suddenly snapped.

Clark had no right to act so superior! She had seen him in similar situations often enough. Their two pairs of blue eyes locked as she returned his furious look with one of her own. Then Trish remembered Jonathan, who was still in his cruiser behind her. She refused to lose her temper in front of Jonathan; she had already made enough of a fool of herself without that.

Trish turned around, taking a deep breath as she did. "Oh, Clark, I'd like you to meet Jonathan Stewart," she said, hoping to defuse Clark's fury through distraction.

"I asked what happened," Clark repeated a little more loudly. Her tactic hadn't worked. If anything, Clark was angrier.

"Jonathan," Trish continued, deciding to ignore Clark's anger, "this is my brother, Clark Everett."

"Glad to meet you, Clark," Jonathan said enthusiastically. "You have quite a reputation around here. In fact, I hope to—" Jonathan stopped abruptly, realizing that Clark wasn't listening.

Instead Clark grabbed Trish's hand and gave it a rough squeeze. "Well?" he hissed, not letting go.

Trish yanked her hand away. "We went over," she said, looking Clark in the eye without blinking. She tried to tell herself that he was the one making a fool of himself, but somehow that didn't help. She still felt embarrassed. He was treating her like a child, and he had to be stopped.

"I gathered that much. *How* did it happen?" Clark looked out at the lake. "It's hardly windy enough to go over while pleasure sailing," he added scornfully.

Taking a deep breath, she said in a calm tone, "I'll tell you what, Clark. I'm going to go take a hot shower. After that, I'll fill out a complete accident report for you. All right?" She pushed her face into his and added, "Hmmmmm?"

Then, before Clark could recover from the shock, Trish stomped past him and up the stairs. She wished that her shoes would clatter on the whitewashed boards instead of squishing. With her heart pounding wildly in her chest, her only thought was to get away from all of them. Then she suddenly remembered that she was wearing Jonathan's shirt.

Turning around, she went back. "Here," Trish said, thrusting the shirt at Jonathan. "And thanks again for all your help."

"My pleasure." Jonathan smiled, revealing a single dimple on his right cheek. Trish turned and fled.

"What do you think of him? Isn't he an absolute doll?" Mary asked later after they had both showered and were sitting on Trish's canopy bed towel drying their hair.

"Who?" Trish asked absently. Now that she had warmed up, she felt incredibly tired.

"Not your brother, that's for sure!" Mary shook

her head. "Was he ever in an ugly mood! What was with him, anyway?"

"I guess he's torn between wanting to go away this summer and wanting to hang on to being skipper of the boat."

Mary laughed. "Well, you certainly showed him up. I thought he was going to explode after you left. His face actually turned purple." Mary giggled. "Luckily, Jonathan handled him well. You know, got him all calmed down. I thought Clark was going to make me stay down there until all the water was out of the boat, but Jonathan insisted I go up and take a hot shower, too. That guy is a dream come true. He's not only cute, but nice, also."

"He's all right, I guess."

"All right?" Mary asked. "You must have gotten hit on the head or something when we went over. He's more than all right. Didn't you see those green eyes? That fantastic, honey-colored hair? That gorgeous smile?"

"You sound as though you're interested in him," Trish said cautiously, handing Mary the comb. If Mary was interested in Jonathan, Trish knew she didn't have a chance with him. Mary was so much better looking than Trish could ever hope to be.

"I'm not thinking of Jonathan for myself!" Mary cried indignantly. "I've got Deke, remember? Jonathan's going to be *your* boyfriend."

Trish pulled her pink, terry cloth robe tighter and shivered. "Oh, sure," she replied with a short laugh. "And it's going to rain roses tomorrow. Mary, he's much too good-looking." Jonathan's green eyes, intense and kind at the same time, flashed in her mind. Having a boy as attractive as Jonathan interested in her was more than Trish had ever dared hope for.

"Don't be silly. I think you're every bit as good-looking as he is, and I could tell that Jonathan thought so, too. In fact, he kept his eyes glued on you until you disappeared at the top of the steps during that dramatic exit of yours. Stomping off like that was so smart. It really got his attention."

"I didn't do it to get his attention," Trish said, remembering how furious Clark had been and how close to tears she had been. "Anyway," she sighed, "he doesn't know my phone number even if he did want to get in touch with me."

"He knows both your first name and your last name. I saw to that. And he seemed to know who Clark was, too. Jonathan didn't leave when I did, you know. He stayed to help Clark clean *Lady* up."

"That hardly means Jonathan will call me," Trish persisted, even though she secretly hoped she was wrong.

"No," Mary agreed, leaning over the side of the bed and picking something up from the floor. "But *this* does."

"That's Jonathan's jacket!" Trish gasped.

Mary nodded. "Right."

"How could you forget to give him back his jacket?" Trish demanded.

Mary's brown eyes sparkled with mischief. "I didn't exactly forget. Let's just call it strategy. You know, a gentle reminder."

"But he'll have to call *you* to get it back, not me. He knows you're the one he gave his jacket to."

Mary shook her head. "I don't have it anymore. I'm leaving it here. He's going to have to call *you* to get it back. And when he does, you can make your move!"

Chapter Two

Thanks to Mary, Trish had Jonathan's jacket, a soft, navy-blue shell with an outer layer of maroon Gortex. Surely he needed his jacket, Trish told herself, but several days had passed, and he hadn't called. She didn't really think he'd ask her for a date just to get his jacket back, but she *had* expected him to make some sort of effort to get it from her.

Looking at the jacket hanging in her closet, Trish tried to imagine how Jonathan could have forgotten about it. Did he have a closetful of jackets just like it, she wondered? If that were the case, he would probably never miss it.

She walked slowly to the closet and took the jacket from its hanger. Glancing toward the door to make sure it was closed, she slipped the jacket on. Its size reminded her that Jonathan was taller than she was. So few boys were!

Trish wanted to leave it on, but she was afraid

someone might see her in it. She knew Clark would tease her unmercifully and would probably get her father to join in, too. With a sigh, she hung the jacket back in the closet. She would have to put Jonathan Stewart out of her mind just as he had obviously put both her and his jacket out of his mind. After all, this was Mary's silly scheme, not hers. Trish had more important things to do anyway. She had to study for her final exams.

The following Saturday Mary came over to help Trish scrub the bottom of the boat. They tipped *Lucky Lady* on her side and rubbed liquid dish soap around the shiny varnish of the nearly flat, wooden bottom. When the subject of Jonathan's jacket finally came up, Mary said, "It's been a week, and this is getting silly. Let's call him."

"Are you out of your mind?" Trish gasped, nearly dropping her scrub brush into the lake. "What will we say?"

"*You'll* say, 'Hi, this is Trish Everett. I have your jacket.' " Mary replied. "That's simple enough, isn't it?"

Trish started scrubbing the boat with renewed vigor. "I don't know his number."

"We'll look it up." Mary tossed her brush into the bucket of sudsy water. "Come on," she said, getting to her feet.

"We can't leave the boat like this," Trish told her, continuing to scrub.

"Sure we can. We'll be back soon." She grabbed

Trish's brush and tossed it into the bucket with her own. "Besides, we're really done, aren't we?"

Trish nodded. "I guess so. Let's pull the boat up again and put it away first."

"All right!" Mary gave her a thumbs-up signal. "You're actually going to do it!"

Trish handed Mary the jib halyard and then took the main halyard for herself. "Do I have a choice?" she asked, bracing herself for the pull.

Working together, they managed to right *Lucky Lady*. The sailboat's flat bottom slapped the water loudly as it landed. Trish then secured *Lady* to the boat lift, and the two girls started up the white wooden steps to the house.

"Where's your phone book?" Mary asked when they reached the porch.

Trish answered, "In the kitchen."

Mary charged ahead. "Come on then. Let's go."

"Wait a minute," Trish said, grabbing hold of Mary's sleeve. "I think I've just changed my mind."

"Well, I haven't." Mary snapped her fingers authoritatively and walked into the kitchen. "The phone book, please."

Reluctantly, Trish pulled it out of a drawer and handed it to Mary. After a few minutes of scanning the page of Stewarts, Trish said, with just a touch of relief in her voice, "There's no listing for a Jonathan Stewart. He was probably just a figment of our imaginations."

"Hardly," Mary retorted, running her own finger down the column. "He wouldn't have his own listing. What's his father's name?"

Trish shrugged. "How should I know?"

"Well, do you know his address?" Mary ran her finger down the page again.

"I'm afraid he didn't tell me that at the same time he didn't tell me his father's name and his telephone number. I think this is hopeless," Trish added just as Clark burst into the kitchen.

"Hi, you guys! What are you up to?" he asked, peering over Mary's shoulder. "Rats! I was hoping you were doing something domestic, like baking cookies."

Trish tried to reach across Mary to slam the phone book shut, but before she could, Mary said, "Maybe you're just the person who can help us, Clark."

Trish wanted to yell, "No, Mary! Don't tell him!" But she wasn't quick enough.

Clark returned Mary's smile. "Sure, I'll help you if I can."

Trish felt her face turn a hundred shades of red as Clark looked thoughtfully at the refrigerator for a second and then said, "What do you want to know?"

Mary began to explain. "I forgot to give Jonathan back the jacket he let me wear. We thought he'd have called us to get it back by now, but he hasn't. So, we thought we'd call him and let him know that we have it."

"All he told me was that he has a sailboat just like *Lucky Lady*, and he's racing it on Sand Lake this summer. He said he had been hoping to take me on, and he was disappointed that I wasn't going to be around this summer. But I assured him that I'd be back to finish the season." Clark paused to wink meaningfully at Trish. "He seemed happy to hear that, and that was about it. He didn't even tell me his last name," Clark answered Mary.

"It's Stewart," Trish said.

"Stewart," Clark repeated thoughtfully. "I don't know. He said he just moved out here April first, so he probably isn't in the book yet. Try information." Reaching in front of Trish, he grabbed an apple from a bowl of fruit on the counter. "Now, why don't you girls bake some cookies?"

"If you want homemade cookies, make them yourself," Mary told him. "We're too busy."

"Figures you'd say that. Where are Mom and Dad, Trish? Do you know?" he asked, his mouth full of apple.

She shook her head. "We've been down on the dock all morning, washing the boat."

"Why?" he asked. "It hasn't had time to get dirty yet, has it?"

"It was dirty enough to need a wash. Anyway, we needed the practice," Trish told him.

Clark chuckled. "I guess you need all the practice you can get, don't you?" He waved his apple at Mary. "Good luck tracking that guy down, Mare."

Mary smiled and batted her long, dark lashes at him again. "Thanks, but I'm not worried. I always get my man."

"How could you?" Trish demanded after she

heard the back door slam and was certain that Clark was out of earshot.

"How could I what?" Mary asked innocently.

"How could you drag Clark into this thing? I don't need him walking around the house making kissing noises."

"Come on, Trish. He's almost seventeen. He's way beyond that."

"That's what you think," Trish retorted.

"Anyway, he didn't suspect a thing. I did all the talking. If he's going to think anyone is interested in Jonathan, he's going to think it's me. Besides, Clark will be going away soon, won't he?" Mary asked, closing the phone book.

"Not soon enough," Trish said.

"Come on, brighten up," Mary coaxed. "We're going to try information. At least Clark helped us that much."

"Not much of a lead after all," Trish said when information failed to locate any new listing for the Stewart family.

"Well, if nothing else, you've got a new jacket," Mary said cheerfully.

"It's too big," Trish admitted gloomily.

"Cheer up. It's only been a week. He's going to call," Mary insisted, putting the phone book back in its drawer.

The following Monday night Trish was in her room supposedly studying for her first final when the telephone rang.

"Trish!" she heard her mother yell a few seconds later. "Telephone!"

"OK," she called back. Rolling lazily across the bed, she picked up the receiver. "Hi," she said casually, expecting the caller to be Mary.

"Hi," a voice too deep to be Mary's said back, catching her totally off guard. "Is this Trish Everett?"

"Yes—ah—I mean, speaking," she answered.

"This is Jonathan. Jonathan Stewart. Remember me?" he added.

"Oh, hi." Her heart started racing at the mention of his name. *He called!* was all she could think. *He really called!*

"Your friend—" he began, but Trish didn't let him finish.

"I know," she broke in. "She gave it to me." She looked at the jacket hanging in her closet. "I mean, I have it here. Your jacket, that is."

"Good." He sounded relieved. "That makes it easier, since I already know where you live."

"Yes," she quickly agreed, anxious to keep up the momentum of their conversation. "I mean, that's what Mary thought. That's why she left it here after she realized she still had it. We tried to find your telephone number to let you know but—"

"We're new out here, so we aren't in the book yet," he finished for her.

"That's what Clark told us."

"I would have called sooner, but school gets pretty hectic at the end of the year."

"Where do you go to school?" she asked. "I don't think I've ever seen you around Sand High."

"I go to Benton Academy. Have you ever heard of it?"

"Of course. Everyone's heard of Benton!" she said, gushing. Immediately she wished that she had simply said yes. Benton might be a well-known private school, but, after all, a school was a school.

When he didn't say anything right away, Trish was afraid she had ruined the flow of their conversation. She wanted to sound cool and sophisticated, or, if not that, she wanted to at least be able to flirt with him. She was finally getting a chance—a chance that her best friend had gone to great lengths to arrange—but a chance nonetheless, and she was blowing it. She tried to think of what Mary would say.

"You probably want your jacket back soon, right?" she asked after a moment.

"It's a great sailing jacket. It stays warm even when it gets wet," he said enthusiastically.

Trish forced herself to chuckle. "Sounds like something I could use."

Her joke seemed to work. He laughed, too. "You aren't planning on taking another plunge until the water's warmer, are you?"

"I hope not," Trish answered. She wished she could say, "Only if you'll promise to be there to rescue me."

"About my jacket—" he began.

"Yes," Trish said anxiously. "How can I get it to you?"

"Are you busy on Friday?"

Friday! She struggled to catch her breath. "Sure," she replied. "I mean, no, I'm not busy," she corrected herself. Maybe he was going to ask her for a date to get his jacket back.

"I get home from school a little after two. If I sail over, I could probably be at your dock around three. Will you be home by then?"

"Sure," she agreed quickly. "I'd like to see your boat. My brother told me you have a scow similar to ours."

"I do, just like yours. The only real difference is the color of the deck," he told her. "So, I'll see you Friday at three, OK?"

"At three," she echoed.

"Well, 'bye then."

" 'Bye." Then she slowly hung up the phone. She knew that between that moment and three o'clock Friday afternoon, she would be mentally replaying their conversation at home, at school, awake, asleep. He had been so easy to talk to. Maybe Mary was right. Maybe Trish *did* have a chance with him.

"Come home with me," Trish pleaded with Mary at lunch on Friday.

"You don't want me there," Mary said, calmly poking her straw into a carton of milk.

"Yes, I do. I wouldn't keep asking you if I didn't. After all, you're the one who kept his jacket."

Mary laughed. "Come off it, Trish. You make it sound as though I kept his jacket for myself. I kept it for you, remember? I kept it just so

33

something like this afternoon would happen. And now that it's happening, you want me to be there to ruin it?"

She deftly scooped up a forkful of mixed vegetables. "I don't think you really do. Remember, 'Two's company; three's a crowd.' " Setting down her fork, she picked up her hamburger and took a huge bite. "Aren't you going to eat?" Mary asked, putting her hamburger down and taking another forkful of vegetables. "This is your favorite school lunch."

"I can barely stand looking at the food much less eating it." Trish disdainfully poked at her apple crisp as if to prove her point.

"You really are a nervous wreck, aren't you?" Mary asked, her voice filled with sympathy.

"That's why I want you to come home with me. That way, *you* can do all the talking."

Mary picked up her milk carton and wagged it at Trish. "Trish, Trish, Trish. You've got to do your own talking. Besides, it sounds as if you did all right on the phone the other night."

"That was just luck." Trish sighed.

"Luck has nothing to do with it. He's a nice guy, and he likes you. Relax, will you?" Mary smiled encouragingly at Trish. "He's coming over to your house this afternoon not only to pick up his jacket, but to show you his boat, right?" Trish nodded. "And then you're going to ask him to come up to your house for a soda, aren't you?"

Trish nodded, even though she hadn't thought of such a thing until Mary mentioned it.

"This is definitely a start," Mary insisted. "A good start."

"Thanks for the pep talk," Trish told her.

"Don't mention it," Mary said, attacking her hamburger again.

At three o'clock that afternoon Trish started down to the dock with Jonathan's jacket and without Mary. Luckily, Clark had gone to the mall with their mother to buy some things he still needed for camp. She tried to find comfort in the fact that if she did make a fool of herself, it would only be in front of Jonathan.

When it got to be five after three and he hadn't shown up yet, she decided he wasn't coming. She scanned the lake for his boat and saw nothing that resembled *Lady* with only one person aboard. *Has Jonathan forgotten,* Trish wondered? *Did he have to stay late at school? Has he changed his mind altogether?*

Just as she was about to start back up the stairs to the house, she heard someone call her name. Turning around, she realized that one of the sailboats she had been watching was Jonathan's after all.

"Trish!" someone called again. As the boat drew closer, Trish saw that Jonathan wasn't alone. *So much for Mary's plan,* she told herself. Then the other boy, whom she didn't recognize, called out, "Trish!" a third time as if they were long lost friends.

Waving, she walked to the end of the dock to

35

catch their boat. Just as Jonathan had said, the only real difference between the two boats was the color of their decks; *Lady*'s was sunshine-yellow, and Jonathan's was the same shade of bright blue as his cruiser.

Trish put her foot out to slow them down, but that proved unnecessary. Jonathan turned into the wind at exactly the right moment and slid gracefully to an almost complete stop just as the bow touched her sneaker.

"Hi, Trish," Jonathan said, looking even more handsome than she had remembered. The sun danced on his hair, showing off its blond highlights, while his eyes, an incredible shade of emerald-green, sparkled with enthusiasm.

"Hey, long time, no see," the other boy said. Turning her attention to him, Trish decided that he did look familiar. His multitude of freckles, and carrot-colored hair topping a tall, lanky body shouldn't have been easy to forget.

"You don't remember me, do you?" the red-headed boy asked, stepping onto the dock. "I'll give you a clue," he began.

"Trish, this is Paul Anderson," Jonathan broke in, stepping onto the dock behind him and resting his hand on Paul's shoulder. "He's crewing for me this summer. I thought we'd get some practicing in today as long as we had to sail over to get my jacket."

"Paul Anderson!" Trish repeated in disbelief. She remember a wiry little redheaded boy, but Paul certainly wasn't little anymore. He seemed magnified—even his face was larger, squarer, and more freckled than ever.

"You remember me now, don't you?" Paul demanded, grinning widely.

Trish nodded. "Sure. How are you? You haven't been around the yacht club for a couple of summers, have you?"

Paul shook his head. "No. I'd decided to give up sailing, but Jonathan talked me into taking it up again." Then he added, "I've changed, haven't I?" Before she could answer, though, he said, "But then, so have you. For the better, too." He eyed her appraisingly.

Jonathan stepped around Paul. "I'm really glad to be getting my jacket back. It's been a cold week without it."

Thankful for Jonathan's intervention, Trish handed him the jacket. She had planned on saying, "It's been in good hands." With Paul around, though, she couldn't bring herself to say it.

"Thanks for taking care of it for me," Jonathan added. He seemed to be waiting for something. Perhaps, Trish thought, *an invitation to stay a little longer.*

Trish took a deep breath. "Are you guys in a hurry?"

Jonathan shrugged. "No, not really. Why?"

"Want to come up to the house for a soda?"

Jonathan turned to Paul. "Is that OK with you?"

Paul giggled. "Sure, why not. I've never seen the famous Everett house before. You know, it's the home of Sand Lake's one and only Clark Everett."

"Come on then," she said, turning and starting toward the steps that led up the steep bank of Sand Lake to the house.

"By the way, is your brother around?" Jonathan asked when they got up to the yard.

"No, he went to the mall to get some things for camp. They sent a whole list of gear he has to have with him. I guess the summers are even colder in Maine than they are here in Minnesota."

"That's too bad. I was kind of hoping he might like to look over my boat," Jonathan said. "Maybe next time. When is he leaving for camp?"

"The Monday after the first races," she answered. It began to seem to Trish that Jonathan had sailed over to see Clark instead of her. "I'll get the stuff and bring it out," she added, pointing to a group of lawn chairs that overlooked the lake. "I'll only be a minute."

When she got inside, she let out a deep breath. Nothing was going according to plan. She wished Mary had come home with her. Mary could handle just about any boy. Sighing, Trish got three cans of soda out of the refrigerator and put them on a tray along with a bag of pretzels and started back outside.

"Thanks," Jonathan said when she handed him the first can. "You've got a great view of the lake up here."

Trish nodded. "Thanks. I love looking at it."

"Where's your crew today?" Jonathan asked, taking a handful of pretzels from the bag.

Trish handed Paul his soda. "She had to study. We've got finals next week."

"We do, too," Paul said as he popped the top of his can. "I'll be glad when they're over."

"Paul goes to Benton with me," Jonathan explained. "We've been friends since kindergarten."

Paul nodded. "And now we're neighbors, too."

"Your brother told me that you're skippering *Lucky Lady* and Mary's going to crew for you," Jonathan commented. "I admit, I was disappointed that I wouldn't be able to race Clark, but now I'm looking forward to taking you on."

Paul seemed to choke on the pretzels he'd been chewing. *"You're* going to skip the boat this summer? All summer long?"

Trish found herself wishing his choking had been more serious. "Yes. At least for the first eight weeks while Clark's at camp."

Jonathan looked over at Paul. "I told you that."

"I know you did, but I didn't believe it. Don't you know what they call this woman on Sand Lake?" Trish gritted her teeth. She wished she could stop Paul, but she couldn't think of anything to say. When no one said anything, Paul went on. "They call her 'Terrible Trish.' She's only skipped the boat a few times, but she nearly sank several boats each time she did."

"That's an exaggeration!" Trish cried in her own defense. "I had a couple of minor collisions, that's all."

Paul started to chuckle, and it turned into a

full-fledged belly laugh. "There are always two sides to a story, I guess," he said when he had calmed down enough to talk.

"I'd like to hear your side, Trish," Jonathan said, getting to his feet. "It will have to be some other time, though. I've got to run some errands before dinner."

"I've got stuff to do, too," Paul said, looking at his watch. "Besides, it looks as if the wind's dying down, and it could take us awhile to get home. Well, nice to see you again, Trish. Say hi to your brother for me."

Trish nodded. "I will." She tried not to let her anger show. Paul had succeeded in making her look like a fool in front of Jonathan. First Clark and now Paul! She was sure that if things continued the way they were going, Jonathan would think she was a complete idiot soon.

"Thanks again for taking such good care of my jacket," Jonathan said as the three walked over to the steps going down to the dock.

"Anytime," she told him sincerely. Then she stayed at the top of the steps and watched them climb down. Silently she said goodbye to the gorgeous boy with the dazzling green eyes. She had known from the beginning that she didn't have a chance with him. How had she ever let Mary convince her she did?

Once on the dock, Jonathan turned around. "See you soon," he called back up the steps to her.

Soon! The word echoed in her ears. What did he mean by that, she wondered? Was he actually planning on seeing her again? There were only two weeks of school left until summer vacation began. Would she be spending time with him during that vacation?

Trish watched them board Jonathan's boat and push off from the dock. As the boat swung around, she read the name: *Lightning*, And, just like lightning, it struck her that the first yacht club race was only two weeks away. Of course he'd see her soon—at the starting line!

Chapter Three

When Trish woke up the Saturday morning of the first race, she leaped out of bed and ran to her window. A quick look outside confirmed her worst fears: the wind was even stronger than the one that had tipped them over a couple of weeks earlier. It blew so hard that the thick, gnarled oak tree in the yard was swaying as though it were a poplar.

As she watched the trees outside her window move, her mind replayed the whole horrible capsize, the cold water and, even worse, the incredible helpless feeling she had had. She wished she hadn't so stubbornly refused to perform the capsize drills Clark had repeatedly suggested. If she couldn't right the boat in the middle of an empty lake, how was she ever going to right it during a crowded race?

Trish wanted to go back to bed and stay there.

Only the thought of Clark saying, "I told you so!" made her get up and walk into the bathroom.

After washing up, Trish slipped into a pair of heavy canvas shorts and a matching blue sweatshirt and went downstairs. She was getting so worried about the race that even the thought of seeing Jonathan again failed to make her feel any better.

Trish walked into the kitchen and found Clark eating enough breakfast for an army. "Pretty windy out there," he said, without looking up from his plate of sausages and eggs. "Sure you can handle it?"

Her head cleared slightly. "Of course I can. Why do you ask?" She wasn't about to give Clark the satisfaction of knowing that she had any doubts at all.

Clark looked up and eyed her carefully. "I just thought you might want me to skip the boat for you today. As long as I'm still here and everything."

Part of her, probably the sensible part, longed to scream, "Yes, yes, yes!" But she wasn't about to give in to that voice, sensible or not. "Oh, no," she said instead. "I can handle it."

He shrugged, turning his attention back to his breakfast. "Suit yourself, but I'm not doing anything today if you change your mind."

It was possible that Clark was just being thoughtful, and Trish decided to give him the benefit of the doubt. "Thanks," she said, casually picking out an orange from the bowl of fruit on the counter and sticking her fingernail into it to peel it. "Do you know where Mom and Dad are?"

"Mom went shopping, I think. Dad's working on the hedge. Why?" He looked up expectantly.

"No reason," she responded. Then she gave him what she hoped was a mysterious smile and strolled confidently out of the kitchen. But as soon as she was in the hallway, a new wave of apprehension rippled through her. Looking at the orange she was clutching in her hand with distaste, Trish quickly threw it in a waste-basket in the front hall.

She looked at the door for a moment, considering whether or not to search for her father for a possible heart-to-heart discussion, but decided against it. Trish already knew he'd say, "Do your best, Trish. That's all anyone can do." But he would really mean, "Get out there and win! It's the Everett way!"

Some comfort! Her father would be thinking about winning, about adding another trophy to the family case, while she would be worrying about survival.

By the time Mary arrived, the wind was literally howling. "Do you think they'll call off the race?" Mary asked as soon as she stepped in the door. "I don't think I can take another plunge in that icy water."

Seeing Mary in such a nervous state made Trish feel worse. Surely if Mary knew how scared Trish was, she would simply refuse to go out at all.

Trish forced herself to smile. "It's the fifteenth

of June," she said cheerfully. "The water is *much* warmer than it was three weeks ago."

"How much warmer?" Mary asked doubtfully.

Trish waved her arm in the general direction of the lake. "Look, this isn't bad. This is exciting. This is what inland-lake racing is all about. Ask Clark. Besides," she added, "if we do go over for some reason, we'll be surrounded by people to help us if we need it."

Mary's voice picked up a little as she asked, "Is Clark going to sail with us?"

It dawned on Trish that in such a heavy wind, they probably did need a third person on the boat to keep it from riding too high in the water. Even if Trish and Mary could keep it from going over, they'd have a hard time moving at any speed if they had to keep letting wind out of the sail to bring the boat back down to a position that was steerable. Why shouldn't that third person be Clark? It would certainly be easier to ask him than to find someone else on such short notice.

"Maybe," Trish answered. "Let's go ask him."

Her intuition told her it was about time for him to be back in the kitchen eating again, and she was right. Clark was in the same spot he'd been in a few hours earlier, this time devouring a massive peanut butter sandwich.

"Hey," Clark said when he saw them. "How's it going?"

"That looks great!" Mary cried out before Trish could ask him anything. "I'm famished!"

"Help yourself," Clark offered gallantly, indicating the still-open jar of peanut butter on the counter.

Mary took out a couple of slices of wheat bread for a sandwich. Since food was the last thing on Trish's mind, she just stood there trying not to gasp for air as her chest contracted with fear.

"There's still time to reconsider," Clark said between bites.

"Reconsider what?" Mary asked, plunging the knife into the peanut butter.

"I offered to skip the boat today. I thought Trish might not be up to tackling this heavy wind. Want some soda?" he added, extending a half-full bottle toward the girls.

Trish shook her head. There was less than an hour until the start of the race. She was tempted to let him skip. After all, if she was crewing, she could devote her full attention to looking for Jonathan. But what would Jonathan think if he saw her crewing instead of skipping, she asked herself? He'd undoubtedly think that Paul had been right, that Trish was a loser. A boy like Jonathan wouldn't be interested in a loser. She had to show them all that they were wrong about her. Trish knew she had to skip the boat, and she had to do well, or she could forget about Jonathan Stewart.

"Well?" Clark pressed.

"The answer is no," Mary replied firmly before Trish could get out the words. "You can crew with me if you like, though. Can't he, Trish?"

Bolstered by Mary's show of confidence, Trish said, "But I have to know right away. I'll have to start making phone calls if you're not interested."

Clark shrugged. "Sure. Why not? I'm not doing anything else today." He smiled and gave his sister a friendly wink.

Trish decided that he wasn't really trying to give her a hard time. He simply wanted to be out on the boat for the race.

"Good," she said. "That'll be great."

She pulled out one of the white kitchen chairs and sat down with Clark and Mary. Both of them seemed to be putting away massive amounts of food. Looking out the window toward Sand Lake, she could see her father digging weeds out of the flower bed that topped their steep bank. For everyone else it was business as usual. Only Trish was trembling.

She tried to imagine what Jonathan was doing at that moment. Was he eating? Or was he working on his boat, scrubbing algae off the smooth, varnished surface? She could almost see the sun gleaming in his streaked hair as he bent over his task. She could even imagine him whistling as he sprinkled cleanser on his sponge.

"Well, I'm full," Clark announced, bringing her pleasant daydream to an abrupt halt. "Let's go down and rig the boat."

Mary got to her feet. "I'm ready."

Trish found herself trailing after them to the dock. She wanted to yell, "Hey, I'm the skipper!" but she realized that she would sound ridiculous. They knew she was the skipper. She was the one who was having a hard time believing it, and until she did, she would have a hard time giving the others orders.

"Good luck!" her father called cheerfully, waving a pair of lawn clippers at them as they passed. "Don't forget to wear your life jackets. Looks like a day when you might get wet."

"We aren't going to tip over, are we?" Mary asked as they started down the steps to the dock.

"I hope not," Trish told her. "It isn't what I have in mind. But, if we do, we can handle it, right?"

"That's right," Clark assured Mary, resting his hand protectively on her shoulder. "I'm here now."

"Oh, brother!" Trish groaned.

"At least I have boat shoes today," Mary said. Everyone looked down at her feet. The clunky, thick-soled shoes gleamed. "I should be able to bounce on the boards now without slipping off— if we have to."

"You have an intelligent, responsive crew here, Trish," Clark said. "I hope you appreciate that."

"I do," she assured them both. "And to prove it, I'll get the sails out of the shed, while you two get the boat off the lift." Then she added, "OK?"

Clark put three fingers to his temple and saluted. "Aye, aye, skipper."

He had a little smirk on his face that Trish didn't like at all. As she opened the door to the shed, she couldn't help wondering if it was a mistake to have brought him along. If the wind would just die down, she could *un*invite him.

Unfortunately, the reverse was happening. The wind seemed to be picking up. Trish pulled the mainsail bag off its hook and felt her stomach do a double flip. Then, after getting the jib, which was wound around its small sticklike boom, she took a deep breath and boldly left the shed. Sails in hand, Trish returned to her eager crew.

"Here," she said, tossing the sail bag to Clark. "You thread the mainsail." Then she handed the rolled-up jib to Mary. "And you take care of this."

Even rigging the boat in such a strong wind was difficult. Every time the mainsail trapped a little wind, the boom snapped across the boat like a cannonball. It was the kind of wind that caused people to get hurt and boats to collide.

Her nervousness increased with these thoughts, and she began having trouble breathing. If Clark and Mary knew she lacked confidence, they might decide not to let her skip after all. But, finally, everything seemed to be in order. Clark hoisted the jib and pushed them away from the dock. Apparently, she thought, the others had been too busy to notice her nervousness.

Immediately, a gigantic puff of wind blew past them, sending the boat heeling up on its side. They quickly found the canvas hiking straps and leaned out over the water to counteract the tipping action caused by the wind. Trish found her fear turning into exhilaration as *Lady* skimmed across the surface of the lake, cutting into the whitecaps. She had never seen Clark hike out so far. Clearly, his weight was keeping them at a perfect angle.

I can do it! I can do it! she told herself over and over again until she began to actually believe it.

They practiced a few maneuvers. During the last one, Trish was deciding where Clark and Mary would sit and who would be responsible for which tasks when Clark announced that he would sit in the middle and handle the boards and the side stays; Mary would handle timing the start with the stopwatch, holding the jib, and making adjustments to the pocket of the sail. Trish knew Clark was right, that his greater weight should be toward the stern, but she didn't like the fact that he had made the decision for her.

Trish was about to argue with him when she spotted the judges' boat. From the flags they were flying, she saw that the race would be twice around a triangular course. They sailed to the starting line. Clark could stay where he was because she didn't have time to assert herself as skipper by changing seating arrangements that were right in the first place.

Even though Trish and her crew were early, several other boats were also at the starting line. She could see the rest of the fleet heading out from the yacht club, which was located on an island accessible only by boat. *Lucky Lady*'s class would start first since there were more boats in it than in the rest of the classes combined.

They practiced their approach to the line a few times before the judges fired the ten-minute gun. As soon as it sounded, Clark began offering suggestions about where Trish should be when the race started. She was more than willing to do whatever Clark said. Because of the intensity of the wind, everything was happening much too fast, and she felt as though she were in a daze. Trish wanted to look for Jonathan's boat, but the starting-line crunch was much too intense for her to pay attention to anything but the crunch itself.

When the five-minute gun went off, Mary reported that the stopwatch she was monitoring was right to the second. Clark suggested Trish get as close to the starboard end of the starting line as she could and stay there, letting the sails luff. Seeing that as not only good strategy but also a chance to take a breather, Trish complied.

Trish was just about to head the boat into the eye of the wind when she heard someone call, "Hey there, *Lucky Lady!*"

Jonathan waved as he whizzed by, his boat clearly living up to the name *Lightning*.

"Who was that in Jonathan's boat?" Mary asked, leaning toward Trish from her position on the other side of Clark.

"Paul, I suppose," Trish answered. She had been too busy looking first at Jonathan and then at *Lightning* to notice much of anyone or anything else.

"Trish!" Clark yelled. "Pay attention! We're about to go over the line!" He glared at her accusingly. "You're about to lose our excellent position!"

"How much time do we have?" she asked Mary. Hard as it was, she had to forget about Jonathan, at least for the time being. She reminded herself that she was skipper, and that meant she was responsible for the well-being of both her boat and her crew.

"Two minutes," Mary answered.

Clark shook his head. "Too much time. Fall off and try to come back," he ordered, taking charge, all pretense of making "suggestions" gone. It was no time for resentment, however, and Trish did what Clark told her to do. She even considered handling the tiller over to him, but it was really too late. Pushing the tiller hard to the right to recover the wind made the boat swing around slowly.

"One minute," Mary reported.

Just as the sails were filling with air, *Lightning* came into view again. Trish couldn't resist looking at Jonathan, his sun-streaked hair flowing back in the wind. His tan was already impressive even though it was only June.

"Trish! Look out!" Clark screamed.

She saw the racing committee's temporary buoy just in time to narrowly avoid hitting it. Clark scowled at her. The race hadn't started yet, and she had almost gotten them disqualified! Trish had to forget about *Lightning*, or she could forget about the race. It was clear that she couldn't be thinking about both without getting into trouble.

"Thirty seconds," Mary said, gazing intently at the stopwatch in her hand. Trish doubted if Mary had even seen Jonathan's boat the second time.

Trish looked at the starting line. It seemed as if they could easily slip into the position they'd occupied before their near accident.

"Coming about!" Trish called. The sails started luffing, and all three of them threw themselves across the cockpit to the opposite side of the boat. As soon as the sails were filled again, the boat reared up as if it were a spirited horse, and they were once again zipping along.

Trish didn't want to be going quite so fast when she reached her place along the starting line, but she didn't know how to slow *Lady* down. The cracking of Dacron sails around her sounded like cannons being fired, and she felt as if she were on a battlefield in the midst of a charge.

"Fifteen seconds," Mary intoned.

Trish tried letting the sails out more, hoping that by having them luff, the boat would continue moving forward but at a slower pace. Suddenly it seemed as though the entire fleet was jockeying for the exact spot she wanted.

"Ten seconds," Trish barely heard Mary say above the roar of the other luffing sails. "Nine, eight, seven—"

"Trish!" Clark screamed once again.

But this time he *was* too late. As soon as he had shouted her name, she heard the sickening thud of wood against wood as they made not so gentle contact with another boat.

Bending down, Trish looked under the sail to see the skipper who had called "Right-of-way!" just before impact, and she found herself staring into a pair of startlingly green eyes. Jonathan Stewart's eyes! Angry sparks seemed to fly from them.

Trish kept staring, hoping somehow that she was wrong, that it wasn't Jonathan she had hit. But it was Jonathan, just as clearly as it was Paul hoisting the black protest flag up their forestay. When the starting gun sounded, it might as well have been Trish's heart exploding.

"Let's just go home," Clark said. "He's got an ironclad case against you, little sister. I'm afraid it's all over."

Trish turned the boat around without saying anything, and the rest of the fleet shot past them. She felt like a little kid who had been waiting in line for candy only to find out that there was none left. Now that she couldn't race, she wanted to race more than ever. Even the heavy wind seemed like nothing compared to her disappointment.

"What were you *thinking* about? Anything?" Clark demanded when they'd gotten away from the starting line. The next class was already preparing to begin its race.

What could Trish say? She couldn't tell him she had been thinking about the very person whose boat she slammed into. Besides, she told herself, it wasn't Clark's business, anyway. He was only there because Trish had asked him to be. Still, she felt she had to say something in her own defense. "I was thinking about the starting line. Everything was happening so fast that— "

Clark didn't let her finish. "How do you expect to race if you can't handle the pressure of the crunch?"

"I'll do all right when I'm following my own strategy instead of foolishly taking the advice of my crew," Trish shot back.

"If you aren't careful, you'll end up sinking my boat and someone else's as well. Who knows what kind of damage you've done today, and this was only the first race." He shook his head disgustedly.

"Look, big shot—" Trish started to say.

"Hey, you two," Mary broke in. "I just want to know what happened? I don't understand why we're going home."

"When you ram another boat, and they have right-of-way, you're disqualified," Clark explained wearily, the fight apparently draining out of him.

Mary smiled. "At least we didn't tip over. Besides, there's always tomorrow, right?"

Trish looked at her best friend, torn between feeling grateful that she hadn't brought up Jonathan in front of Clark and irritated that she didn't seem to realize the magnitude of what had just happened. But Mary had been so caught up in minding the jib and keeping track of the time, Trish thought, that she didn't know whom they'd hit!

Clark shook his head. "I only hope you've learned something today, Trish," he grumbled. "Too much of this kind of thing will be the end of this poor boat." He patted *Lady*'s deck as if to comfort the boat.

"So," Mary said after a few moments of uncomfortable silence, "what time is it, anyway?"

Clark glanced at his wristwatch. "About two-thirty, why?"

"Look on the bright side. Now I have scads of time to get ready for my date tonight." She caught Trish's eye. "Want to come over for a while?"

"No thanks. I need to spend the rest of the day getting my head together for the race tomorrow," Trish answered.

"Think your dad might give me a ride home? My folks said they wouldn't be home until four."

"I'll take you home," Clark offered. "If you're sure you want to go home. I thought you girls would be going to the barbecue at the island this afternoon."

"Deke's picking me up early. We're going out for dinner to celebrate his job at the tennis club. He's going to be the assistant pro this summer." Then Mary added, "But Trish is going to the barbecue, aren't you, Trish?"

Shaking her head, Trish said, "I don't think so."

"Why not?" Mary asked.

"I'm too worn out," Trish answered.

"From what?" Clark asked, laughing. "From *not* racing?"

"She's probably tired from being with you," Mary told him.

"Be nice, Mary," Clark warned as they reached the dock, "or I just might change my mind and make you walk home."

Clark grabbed the dock. Then, hopping off with the painter in hand, he tied *Lady* to the back of the boat lift. "How soon did you want to leave?" he asked, stepping back on the boat to lower the sails.

"After we get this put away?" Mary answered.

"Fine with me," he said.

Trish shifted into automatic pilot as she moved around the boat. She barely heard Clark and Mary's easy banter, which seemed to blend into the sound of the wind.

They were finishing up when Mary said. "I think you ought to go to the barbecue, Trish."

Clark chuckled. "Then you can find out whether or not you put a hole in Stewart's boat."

Now Mary knew. She shot Trish a quick look of complete understanding and snapped back at Clark, "There's no *hole* in this boat, and I'm *sure* the other boat is just fine." Mary started pulling the long, stiff batons out of the deflated mainsail with angry little jerks.

Turning to Trish, Clark said, "I think you're

right to skip the barbecue. It's important that you sort yourself out before you do the same thing tomorrow—and every race for the next eight weeks."

This remark was the last straw. Without another word, Trish turned and fled up the whitewashed steps to the house. She didn't stop until she had reached her room. Then she hurled herself onto her canopy bed. As she burrowed her face into the haven of her ruffled pink pillows, her tears started to flow.

Chapter Four

The first thing Trish noticed when she woke up Sunday morning was the wind—or rather the lack of it. Unlike the first race, the second race promised to be a quiet one. Thankfully, Trish wouldn't need to ask Clark or anyone else to race with Mary and herself. What's more, she felt good because she was certain that she would do better with less wind. Everything had moved too fast the day before, and Trish hadn't had enough time to think in all the confusion. If it hadn't been for her embarrassment at the possibility of seeing Jonathan after the previous day's fiasco, she would have felt downright confident, she decided. As it was, Trish merely allowed herself to feel good. Besides, the races began at ten o'clock on Sundays instead of two o'clock as they did on Saturdays. This left less time in the day for worrying.

* * *

As the fleet clustered around the judge's boat in anticipation of the start of the race, Trish thought everything was just the way it had been the day before—except slower. This time she had no trouble paying attention. What she had trouble doing was getting into a good starting position. She couldn't even decide what a good starting position was. As a result, she crossed the starting line.

During the race *Lucky Lady* continued to trail after the rest of the fleet. It seemed as though little puffs of wind that occasionally appeared to hit the other boats would fizzle out before *Lady* could reach them. As the race progressed, they slipped farther and farther behind.

After they finally rounded the first buoy, Trish let the sail out, and the two girls settled themselves down in the cockpit of the boat.

"What are they doing that we're not doing?" Mary wondered out loud. She made a vague gesture in the direction of the other twenty-four boats in front of them.

"If I knew," Trish told her, "I'd be doing it."

"But you know so much. I mean, you know all the parts of the boat and all that stuff. You know how to set the sails so they don't flap and all."

Trish sighed. "I guess sailing and racing are two different things. To race, you need a strategy."

"Oh," Mary said. After a pause, she continued, "Speaking of strategies, I can't believe that you didn't go to the party yesterday." Trish had been waiting all morning for Mary to say something about the party and was only surprised it had taken her that long to mention it.

"I was just too wiped out to do anything," Trish explained, hoping to end the discussion.

"You're absolutely right," Mary said.

"About what?" Trish asked. They were so far behind, Trish noted, it seemed as though they were a one-boat fleet.

"Strategy *is* your weakness. You've got everything going for you except strategy. You need help." Mary shifted her position a little, and even that slight movement made the nearly stationary boat tremble.

"I was too embarrassed to go to the party, OK? Are you satisfied?" Trish glanced up at the little plastic arrow that topped *Lady*'s thirty-foot mast for a sign that the wind was blowing at all. What she saw didn't look promising.

"Jonathan was undoubtedly there," Mary insisted.

"That's just the point," Trish responded. "I couldn't stand the thought of running into him—again," she added pointedly.

"You could have apologized. Or you could have trivialized the entire incident. You could have said you rammed into him just to get his attention or something."

"*You* could have said something like that, Mary, not me."

Mary shook her head. "Clark went to the party. He wasn't too embarrassed to show *his* face."

"Why should he be embarrassed? He was the champion of our class last year. The accident was *my* fault; it was *my* mistake, not his." Trish tried pulling the sail in a little, but it did no good. They continued to stay virtually motionless. "This is the kind of day that races get canceled," she added.

Mary ignored her comment, as she seemed to be ignoring the fact that they were involved in a race. "What did Clark say about the party, anyway? Did he mention anything about Jonathan?"

"Let's try sitting on the low side. Maybe if we change the angle of the boat, we'll catch a little wind." Trish eased herself up on the deck. Mary followed her topside and asked her questions again.

"All Clark said was that it was a good party, and I should have gone. He said we both should have gone."

Mary shook her head. "And I bet you didn't ask him for any details, did you?"

"I don't want Clark to think I'm interested in Jonathan! You don't have an older brother, so you don't know how it feels to be teased by one." Trish wished she could change the subject; she wished she were the one who was leaving for eight weeks the following morning instead of Clark.

"Well, if you keep your feelings for Jonathan a total secret, you can't expect anything to come of them, you know. I think you're entirely too sensitive. Where's your sense of humor, anyway?" Mary demanded.

"*My* sense of humor is fine. Anyway, my feelings aren't a total secret. *You* know how I feel."

"What good does that do? You won't take my advice, and you barely let me help you."

"We're almost at the next buoy," Trish broke in. "It's time for you to reset the mainsail. It's also time to start worrying about getting lapped."

"Good grief!" Mary cried with genuine alarm. "What's that?"

"It means that the other boats in our class will pass us and finish the race before we even start the last lap," Trish explained, glancing nervously behind them. "It's worse than just losing," Trish added. "It's even worse than being disqualified." Besides, she noted silently, it looked as though Jonathan's was the first boat, and he was closing in on *Lady* fast.

Mary moved quickly to the mast and deftly reset the pocket of the sail. They rounded the mark, and, miraculously, a decent-size puff struck them just as Trish was pulling the mainsail tighter. They wouldn't get lapped after all, but they would almost certainly still come in last!

"That's an improvement over yesterday," Mary said cheerfully after they finally crossed the finish line. "At least we finished."

Trish shrugged. She was still living up to her reputation as "Terrible Trish," and she wasn't happy about it.

"Let's sail over to the yacht club and see what's happening," Mary suggested.

"Let's not," Trish replied without hesitation.

"You've got nothing to be ashamed of," Mary insisted.

Trish pulled the sail in a little bit. "I don't?"

"No. Not if you did your best."

Trish wondered if she had done her best. What was her best, anyway? If Clark and Paul were right in their assessment of her, her best was pretty bad. "I'm too tired to go to the island," Trish told her.

"But they're probably discussing strategies. You could learn something. We both could." Mary paused, and Trish could feel Mary eyeing her, waiting for a reaction. "Besides," Mary added, "it's only one o'clock. Most of the afternoon is free."

Only one o'clock, Trish thought despondently, and only the first weekend of the whole, long summer of racing! What had she gotten herself into? And how was she going to get herself out of it?

"I don't want to go out to the island," she told Mary flatly. "I want to go home." Trish braced herself for further arguing. But Mary surprised her.

"OK." Mary shrugged. "It's up to you."

"Really?"

"Really," Mary assured her. "I was thinking of your love life. If you aren't interested in a certain person any longer, there's nothing I can do about it. I can't force you to accept my strategy; I can't even get you to devise your own."

Trish kept *Lady* sailing in the direction of home, but she didn't know whether to feel better or worse. Somehow, winning the argument with Mary made her feel as if she were even more of a loser.

As planned, Clark left for his camp the following morning. There were three more days of finals at Sand High, but he'd managed to get permission to finish his exams early. Trish had wanted to see Clark off at the airport with her parents, but she had her history final that morning. Instead, they gave her a ride to school on their way to the airport.

"Well, so long," Clark said, giving her a hug.

She hugged him back. "Have a great time at camp." She felt a little wistful now that he was really on his way.

"Have a good time yourself," he said nicely enough. "And don't wreck *my* boat."

That wistful feeling evaporated quickly. Trish snatched up her history book and folder. "It's not your boat!" she shot back.

"Now, now," Mrs. Everett said soothingly. "Let's not start all that again."

"Right," Clark said sarcastically. "Let's be realistic. The possibility of an out-and-out disaster is fairly high, wouldn't you say? Dad, don't you agree?"

Everyone turned toward Mr. Everett. But he simply said, "Goodbye, Trish. We'll see you tonight, honey."

With that, she got out of the car and slammed the door. She wished it had been on Clark's fingers. Better yet, his head.

After the history final, Trish tried to talk Mary

into going home with her, but she already had plans with Deke. She did invite Trish to join them, but Trish didn't want to intrude, so she just accepted their offer to drive her home.

By the time they dropped her off, Trish felt thoroughly depressed. She was all alone with nothing to do. She went into the kitchen and thought about having a snack but decided she wasn't really hungry.

She sat down at the kitchen table and looked out the window at the lake. Trish noticed a nice little breeze blowing. She suddenly realized she could take the boat out—it was hers now. Clark was really and truly gone, and Trish felt she didn't have to answer to anyone except herself. That made her feel much better.

She ran up the stairs and threw on her new bathing suit, a flashy royal blue with diagonal purple and white stripes. An afternoon of sailing and working on her tan sounded wonderful. Trish didn't need to be constantly surrounded by people to be happy, she was an independent person with a mind of her own!

As she reached the dock, Trish heard the sound of water lapping against the wooden pilings. It was a sound that she'd known, and from which she'd drawn comfort, all her life. After lowering the boat and pulling it off the lift, Trish tied it to the dock and went into the boat house for the sails. It dawned on her that this was the first time she had ever decided to go sailing by herself in her entire life!

After she had untied the boat and drifted

away from the dock, she was overcome by a feeling of peace. She was in the right place doing the right thing. *This* was what she'd had in mind when she spoke up back in March. *Lucky Lady* might be a racing boat, but it could be used for other things whether the rest of her family accepted that or not.

The sun was pleasantly warm out on the lake, and Trish stretched out along the deck, spreading her hair out behind her like a blond fan. She was still alone, but she no longer felt lonely.

"*Lucky Lady!*" Trish heard a familiar voice call. She sat up and saw *Lightning* sailing toward her. Jonathan was alone, too. "Hi, there," he said as he got closer.

"Hi," Trish called back.

He looked friendly enough, but she still felt shy because of the collision. Self-consciously, she thought of the swimsuit she was wearing, and a chill ran through her body. She thought longingly of Jonathan's jacket, but, of course, he wasn't wearing it. Like Trish, he was wearing only a bathing suit. She noticed that his tanned skin made his honey-colored hair look lighter and his eyes greener. She only hoped she looked half as good in her own swimsuit as Jonathan looked in his.

"It seems we run into each other a lot," he said and laughed as he sailed in closer. At first Trish thought he was making fun of her, but the tone of his voice didn't sound as though he was mocking her. She smiled and forced herself to chuckle along with him.

"Out pleasure sailing?" he asked, pulling in his sail and heading upwind slightly so they now sailed side by side. Trish nodded. "Me, too. How about a game of sail tag?" he suggested, waving a sponge at her.

She paused. She hadn't played tag since she was a little kid just learning to sail. "Sure," Trish told him finally. "Why not?" After all, what did she have to lose? She had already made a fool of herself in front of him more than once.

She watched as he dipped the sponge into the water. Then he whisked it out and, before she could think about doing anything to stop him, he threw it into the middle of her sail.

"You're it!" Jonathan yelled, coming quickly about and sailing away.

Trish had to retrieve the sponge, which had ricocheted off her sail into the water, before she could go after him. He sailed a little way off and then came about, clearly intending to tease her. If he thought she wouldn't be able to coordinate tagging him with the sponge as he had tagged her, he had another thing coming, Trish told herself.

Trish felt a wave of fury course through her arm as she threw the sponge at him. It made a loud splat as it hit his sail dead center. "*You're* it!" she screamed delightedly, jibing away from him.

Before long they were both as wet as their boats were. "Truce," Jonathan called, waving his black protest flag as if it were a white one. "Meet me at that buoy." He pointed at the orange marker about fifty yards away from them, and, before she could say either "all right" or "no, thank you," he came about and was sailing toward the buoy.

She followed him there, and they both tied their boats to the large iron ring on the top of the buoy. Then he asked her for permission to come aboard her boat.

"Permission granted," she told him, and he stepped from his deck to hers.

"You handle that boat very well," Jonathan complimented her, settling himself on the yellow deck across from her.

"I should. I've been sailing since I was old enough to sit up," Trish retorted hotly. Then she added, "You have a right to sound surprised. I guess I should apologize for running into you on Saturday."

"Apologize?" Jonathan sounded honestly dumbfounded. "That kind of thing is part of racing; it's to be expected. What surprised me was that you dropped out right afterward."

"What else was I supposed to do? You had the right-of-way, didn't you?" She shoved a strand of damp blond hair behind her ear.

"You could have blamed the collision on one of those boats that *you* had right-of-way over. You did have a terrific position. That's why most of the fleet was on top of you, you know. He reached up and pushed his blond hair off his forehead. "Anyway," he went on, "I had to protest you. If I didn't, the boat to my starboard would have knocked me out. I should probably be apologizing to you." He smiled, revealing the dimple Trish found so irresistible. Clearly he was trying to make her feel better. She smiled back.

"I'm surprised your brother didn't tell you all that," he said after a moment.

"Clark doesn't know everything," Trish assured him. "Even though he thinks he does."

"Well, I grew up sailing on little Lake Linda, which I know people out here consider a mere puddle. Everyone in the fleet there has heard about your brother and how he took the Sand Lake championship at fourteen."

He stretched himself out along the deck, putting his hands behind his head. "In fact, it was largely your brother's reputation that convinced me to race on Sand Lake this summer. That and my parents' move."

"I didn't know you used to race on Lake Linda. There are a lot of people on Sand Lake who started sailing on Lake Linda," Trish said, hoping to keep their conversation away from the moment he would make the inevitable comparison between Clark and herself.

Jonathan opened both eyes. "Where did you think I came from?" he asked, the yellow of *Lady*'s deck making his eyes seem more golden than green for a moment, as though they were the eyes of a lion.

Trish shrugged and smiled. "I guess I never really thought about it."

"No one takes Lake Linda seriously out here," Jonathan sighed, looking away from Trish. "We know who your club champion is year after year. But none of you ever bother to find out who *our* champion is. Sand Lake is enormous, but Lake Linda has its challenges, too, you know."

"You were the club champion, weren't you?" Trish guessed when he paused.

Jonathan nodded. "I don't like to brag, but the club there has a lot of excellent and competitive sailors. Winning the championship last year was no piece of cake. I had to work hard for it, and after I did win it, I almost hated to move out here because it was so predictable. It's what everyone on Lake Linda expects, get good and move out to Sand Lake where the real sailors are. But it wasn't that way for me. My folks were the ones who wanted to live in a house where they could see the lake from their front window. They don't even care about sailing themselves. They prefer riding in the cruiser."

Jonathan sat up and ran his fingers through his now dry hair. "I could have stayed with the Lake Linda Yacht Club despite the move. I've got my driver's license and everything. I could have driven back to the city for the races, and I even considered it." He paused, staring dreamily at the large expanse of lake surrounding them. "But then I decided to come out here and prove, once and for all, that Lake Linda produces sailors who are as good as the ones on Sand Lake."

He sat up and studied Trish, his green eyes demanding that she understand this passion of his. "And what happens? Your brother, the Sand Lake champion, runs away." Jonathan made it sound as though Clark had found that Jonathan was coming and had fled to his summer camp in Maine in sheer terror.

"He didn't exactly run—" Trish began, prepared to defend Clark. Whatever else her brother might be, he was no coward.

"It doesn't really matter," Jonathan interrupted, composing himself as he settled back on the boat deck, his flashing eyes returning to their usual serene shade.

Trish looked at him in amazement. She couldn't imagine why he felt the need to prove himself to anyone, much less her brother. As far as she could see, Jonathan was perfect. "You've already proven yourself, haven't you?" Trish asked softly. "You're the champion of Lake Linda. Besides, despite our collision, you came in second Saturday and finished first yesterday. At that rate, you'll be the Sand Lake champion in no time."

He shook his head. "The others probably think both those races were a fluke. I'm sure they feel that if Clark had been skipping *Lucky Lady* he would have beaten me. No offense, of course."

Trish knew she didn't measure up to Clark and was, consequently, no competition for someone with Jonathan's racing experience. Blushing, she softly said, "Of course."

"You're a good sailor," he said quickly, reaching across the cockpit to touch her bare knee. "You just need a few races behind you and some practice in between races." Taking her hand in his, he gave it a squeeze, and added, "I bet there's a tiger sleeping inside of you someplace." Grinning, he let her hand go. "In fact, I got a glimpse of that tiger today while we were playing tag."

Trish tried to smile mysteriously, as though she possessed a great, but undisciplined talent for sailboat racing. She couldn't think about racing, though. All she could concentrate on was the feel of his warm hand first on her knee and then squeezing her hand.

Jonathan continued smiling, and, for an instant, it seemed to her as though the whole world consisted of their eyes, locked together in silent communication.

Then he cried, "Hey!" slapping himself on the forehead with the heel of his hand. "I've got an idea! I don't know why I didn't think of this sooner. Clark's left now, hasn't he?"

"Yes, he left this morning," Trish confirmed, wondering if she had told him that Clark was gone.

"I could coach you," Jonathan went on, sounding more and more excited about the idea. "You know, give you some racing tips. You already know how to sail, but racing is something else entirely, isn't it?"

He laughed a joyous laugh, sounding excited by the apparent challenge of this idea. "You can't really expect to *win* the first race you enter, no matter what kind of a sailor you are. You need strategy."

Trish couldn't help wishing Mary were there to hear him say that.

His enthusiasm was infectious. "Yes! I do need a strategy," she agreed.

"Who knows?" he demanded, sitting up again and planting his hands on his bare knees. His face was so close to hers, she couldn't breathe. "You might even turn out to be the competition I lost when your brother left town."

Trish had wanted to say yes, but something in his latest statement stopped her. She wanted to win, but she didn't want to be a replacement for Clark in Jonathan's eyes. Trish wanted to be a competitor in her own right.

"Well . . ." she hedged, leaning away from him. "Let me think about it, OK?"

"We could start right away," Jonathan went on as if she'd said yes instead of maybe. "I'll bet we could even accomplish a lot before the next race."

"How often would we get together? What time and all? I have one more final before I'm through with school," she added.

"I'm done. I finished up last week. But I do have a morning job that starts next week. We'll have to play it by ear, I guess." He looked disappointed. "Look, I can't force you to accept racing lessons from me, I guess. But I do know we'd both enjoy it. Well, you think about it and get back to me. OK?"

"Sure," Trish answered, wondering as she did why she was putting him off. She wanted to spend time with him even more than she wanted to be a better racer, and he was offering her the chance to do both. Why hadn't she simply accepted? But then why was he doing it? Both questions troubled her.

Jonathan got up, and, pulling *Lightning* closer to *Lady*, he boarded his own boat. "Call me and let me know, OK?"

Trish nodded. Suddenly her damp swimsuit felt uncomfortable. She was chilly, and goose bumps covered her bare legs and arms.

Jonathan untied Trish's boat and gave her a shove backward. "So long," he called as the wind filled Trish's sail and she glided away.

" 'Bye," she called back over her shoulder. But Jonathan was busy setting sail himself and didn't seem to hear her.

Trish pulled in the sails and headed for home. She had to call Mary right away. Mary would know what she should do about the lessons, or at least talking with her might clear her own thinking. Then she'd call Jonathan and—

Suddenly she remembered she didn't know his telephone number or his address or his father's first name. How was she going to call him without his number? And when Trish didn't call him, he was bound to think her answer was no. *It's OK*, she told herself as she approached the dock. *Mary will know what to do.*

Chapter Five

Trish called Mary as soon as she got in the house, but Mary wasn't home. She was playing tennis with Deke just as she had said. So Trish left a message with Mary's mother to call her as soon as she walked in the door. "It's urgent!" she told Mrs. Baily.

It was nearly time for dinner before Mary returned her call. "What's wrong?" Mary asked, sounding out of breath. "Clark didn't miss his plane, did he?"

Trish couldn't help laughing. "No, it's nothing like that."

"Then what is it? You aren't sick, are you?"

"Nothing's wrong," Trish assured her. "At least not yet."

"What was so urgent then?" Mary asked, sounding a little irritated.

"It's kind of involved," Trish answered, glancing nervously at her mother who was busily shredding lettuce into a wooden salad bowl. She didn't want to go into the whole thing about Jonathan with her mother listening. "Can you hold on while I run upstairs and get it in my room?"

"I guess so," Mary snapped. "Only try to make it fast, OK? Deke's in the den watching the news with my dad, and I don't want to leave the two of them alone together for too long."

"I'll run," Trish assured her. Then she turned around to where her mother was working. "Will you hang up the phone for me after I get it upstairs?" she asked.

"Yes." Her mother nodded without looking up. "Only, don't make it a long one. We'll be eating in ten minutes, and I want you to set the table."

"It'll be a short one, I promise," Trish said, dropping the receiver on the counter and dashing to the stairs.

"I've got it, Mom," Trish said as soon as she had picked up the phone in her room.

"Remember—" her mother started, but Trish cut in.

"I'll keep it short," she said. Then the phone clicked, and she knew her mother had hung up.

"So, what is this all about? What's the big mystery?" Mary still sounded irritated.

"Well, I took the boat out this morning," Trish began. "And you'll never guess who I ran into."

"Jonathan Stewart," Mary said right away. She didn't sound the least bit surprised, either.

But Mary's tone didn't stop Trish. Quickly shifting gears, Trish said, "Right. Anyway, we played this game of tag, and Jonathan — "

"You what?" Now Mary sounded surprised.

"Tag," Trish repeated. Mary was making it difficult for her. She took a deep breath and said a little more patiently, "We played tag. But that's not the important part." They didn't have much time to talk, and Trish needed to get Mary's feedback on the situation.

"What *is* important," Trish went on, stretching out on her bed, "is that he wants to give me sailing lessons. Well, not sailing lessons exactly, more like racing lessons. I said that I'd think about it and call him. What do you think? Do you think taking lessons from Jonathan is a good idea?"

"I think you're crazy!" Mary practically shouted. "Of course it's a good idea. It's a *terrific* idea, one *you* should have suggested if he hadn't. Deke's giving me tennis lessons, and it's wonderful! My mom's so pleased I'm taking up tennis that she invited Deke to dinner. And, the best part of all is that he accepted. As I told you already, he's in the den watching television with my dad. It's as if he's part of the family instead of 'that boy you see too much of.' "

"But it's different with you and Deke," Trish insisted. "He was your boyfriend before you started the lessons."

"True," Mary conceded. "But that doesn't mean that the whole thing can't work in reverse. Giving you lessons might push Jonathan into being your boyfriend. Besides, you *need* lessons."

"Thanks," said Trish, sitting up and pulling a pillow into her lap. "Thanks a lot." She had called Mary for romantic advice, not sailing advice.

"Come on. Don't get sensitive on me. You know what I mean. Sure you know how to sail, but you don't know how to race. Look, at the very least, you'll be spending time with a great-looking powerhouse of a guy while learning some badly needed racing strategy. At the very most—well, use your imagination!"

Trish used her imagination, and she liked what she saw: Jonathan and herself gliding across Sand Lake at twilight in his blue cruiser on their way to—

"Well, are you going to do it?" Mary demanded.

"Yes," Trish answered firmly. "I'll do it."

"Good," Mary told her. "You know, you couldn't ask for a better way to get to know the guy."

"Yes, I could," Trish assured her. "I'd rather get to know him on a date or even playing sail tag. That wasn't romantic, but it was fun. Suppose I get even worse with lessons. Suppose—"

"Look," Mary broke in, "I've got to go."

Trish sighed, rolling onto her stomach and switching the phone from one ear to the other. "I've got to go, too. And thanks. I guess you're right."

"Of course I'm right. Lessons can only be a good thing for you. I'll talk to you tomorrow," she added. " 'Bye."

Seconds after they hung up, Trish's enthusiasm died when she remembered once again that she still didn't know Jonathan's telephone number. It was all Trish could think about during dinner. The only solution she could think of was to call Paul. If she was lucky, he'd just tell her the number. But Paul would probably ask why Trish wanted it, and if she told him, he might tease her about needing lessons. This was clearly not the best idea, but what choice did she have? Then, there was the next phone call, the one to Jonathan himself. That one would be even harder because it was the one that really mattered.

After dinner her father announced that he was going to the shopping mall to pick up a new suit he was having altered. Jumping at the chance to postpone her phone calls, Trish asked if she could ride along.

"I'd like some company," her father told her.

When they got to the mall, her father asked Trish if she wanted to go to the department store with him or if she wanted to meet him in half an hour. "By the bird cage in the courtyard," Mr. Everett told her when she said she'd meet him later.

Trish went right to the bird cage and sat down. Shopping was the last thing she wanted to do. While watching the little yellow finches hop from perch to perch, she decided not to take lessons after all. Then she wouldn't have to call Paul to get Jonathan's number because she wouldn't be calling Jonathan. Trish would simply tell him no the next time she saw him. Glancing at the large clock on the other side of the cage, Trish saw that only ten minutes had passed. Maybe she'd do a little shopping after all. That was better than agonizing over a couple of phone calls for another twenty minutes, she told herself.

She was on her way to the bookstore when she thought she heard someone call out her name. She looked around to see who it was and found herself staring right into Jonathan Stewart's green eyes.

"Jonathan," she said in surprise. For some reason, he was the last person she had expected to see.

"Hi," Jonathan said, sounding genuinely pleased to see her.

"Hi," Trish replied, equally pleased to see him. "I was just thinking about you," she told him easily.

"That's funny because I was just thinking about you," he responded. He pivoted and began walking in the same direction she was. "Where are you headed?"

"I was going to the bookstore," Trish told him.

"I was planning to go there after hitting the record store, but I could go there now. Mind if I join you?" Jonathan asked.

It was more than fine with her. "Not at all, but I have to meet my dad back at the bird cage in"—she paused to check the clock—"fifteen minutes."

"I've got an idea. I'll meet him with you, and we can ask him if I could drive you home. That way, we can get ice cream or something and talk, OK?"

"OK," Trish said quickly. Then she added, "But what about the bookstore?"

"We'll go there after we meet your father," Jonathan said.

They walked back to the bird cage, and he sat down on one of the wooden benches that surrounded the cage. "We could skip the bookstore altogether tonight and go there another time," he added as Trish sat down next to him.

As they waited, Trish thought there was a good chance her father would say no to the whole idea. Jonathan was telling her a story about his first racing season on Lake Linda, but Trish could barely listen because as the time passed her worry increased. Sitting there with him was so natural and casual, and it would surely ruin everything if her father wanted her to go straight home.

"There you are," her father called from the escalator as he descended into the central courtyard of the mall. "I got my suit," he added cheerfully, shaking a black plastic bag that hung from a heavy wooden hanger.

Trish stood up. She could feel her cheeks growing hot as she faced her father. "Dad, this is Jonathan Stewart."

"Hello, Mr. Everett," Jonathan said, stepping forward, his hand extended for a handshake.

Her father shook Jonathan's hand. "Jonathan," he said. "I've been hearing your name quite a bit lately." Mr. Everett made it sound as if Trish had been talking about Jonathan to her parents! Trish felt her face burn at the thought of what Jonathan must think.

"Good things, I hope." Jonathan laughed good-naturedly.

Mr. Everett nodded. "Very good things. The word's out that you're an excellent sailor."

"Thank you," Jonathan replied.

Mr. Everett then turned to Trish. "I take it you're ready to go home now?"

"Actually," she began cautiously, as nervous as though she were starting a race in a heavy wind, "I thought I'd—"

But before she could finish, Jonathan rescued her by saying, "I offered to drive Trish home, Mr. Everett. If you don't mind, that is."

"Don't you have a final tomorrow?" Mr. Everett asked Trish.

"No. Not until Wednesday," she answered hopefully.

"Then I suppose it's all right," her father said. "But be home by ten."

"I'll have her home before ten, Mr. Everett. I have some studying to do myself," Jonathan told him.

Mr. Everett smiled. "See you both later, then."

After her father had walked away, Trish said, "I thought you were finished with school for the summer."

"I am," Jonathan replied. "But I still have studying to do. I got a stack of sailing books from the library this afternoon, and I'm anxious to look them over. Now, where shall we go?"

"Let's go to the Rainbow and get a cone," Trish suggested.

"I hear they have some pretty wild flavors," he said, waiting for Trish to step on the escalator ahead of him. "I've heard about the place, but I've never been there."

"It's good," she conceded. "Especially if you like exotic flavors."

Jonathan opened the door of the ice-cream store for Trish and followed her to the counter. "What'll it be?" he asked. "My treat. The sky's the limit." He pulled a wad of bills out of his pocket, then added, "Well, almost the limit."

"I just want a single scoop of vanilla," Trish told the girl behind the counter. "In a sugar cone."

"A girl of simple tastes," Jonathan said to Trish. "I like that."

The counter girl handed Trish her cone, then turned to Jonathan. "What will you have?" she asked.

"The same. Only make mine a double."

"You're ordering vanilla, too?" Trish asked while the girl fixed his cone.

Jonathan grinned. "It's my favorite. Sometimes I get talked into trying other flavors, but I always regret it." Jonathan took his cone from the counter girl and handed her a couple of dollar bills. "Most of the girls I know are big on weird flavors like rum bubble and banana-coffee-nut."

Trish shuddered. "Yech!"

He directed her to one of the small tables that lined the far wall. "My sentiments exactly," he said as they sat down.

After taking a few self-conscious licks, Trish felt Jonathan watching her, but she chose not to look back at him. Now that she didn't have to call Paul after all and her worries about her father were gone, Trish knew she ought to be able to relax and enjoy herself. For some reason she couldn't, though.

"You know, we have a lot in common," Jonathan said finally, breaking the silence that had fallen between them.

Trish looked up. Jonathan was smiling at her, his eyes the warm green of pine trees in the summer sun. Trish nodded, even though she wasn't sure what else they had in common beyond liking vanilla ice cream and sailing.

"You're the first girl I've ever met with a passion for sailing. Your brother told me you demanded to race the boat this summer even though he tried to talk you out of it. I admire that, Trish."

"You talked with my brother?" she asked, forgetting to turn her cone to lick the other side. She felt a cold dribble of it hit her hand.

"At the barbecue on Saturday. He came over to apologize for bumping into my boat, I guess." Suddenly he looked at her cone. "Here's a napkin for that drip."

She took the napkin and blotted up the ice cream that was collecting on her hand. "Thanks," she said, blushing.

"Have you had any time to think about those lessons I mentioned?" He leaned toward her, and Trish thought his eyes might melt her ice cream.

"I really do need lessons," Trish confessed. "And how can I pass up free ones from the Lake Linda champion?"

"Now you're talking. When can we start?" Jonathan leaned even closer to her.

"I have my last final on Wednesday morning," Trish answered.

"How about Wednesday afternoon then. At about three o'clock?" Jonathan asked, sounding as anxious for their lessons to begin as she was.

Feeling as if they'd made their first date, she nodded. "That sounds great."

Then he asked, "Do you think your crew could come, too?"

"Mary?" Trish asked, hearing the disappointment in her own voice. She had hoped the two of them would be alone.

"You should have your regular crew with you during a lesson. Racing is a team effort."

"I'll certainly ask her. But I do know that besides sailing with me, she's taking tennis lessons this summer. I wouldn't be too surprised if she couldn't make it," Trish told him.

"I'll bring Paul with me just in case," Jonathan said.

Remembering the last time he had brought Paul with him, she wished she could shout, "Don't do that!" But Paul was Jonathan's friend and his crew, and she couldn't insult him. She just nodded.

Trish finished her cone, and Jonathan said, "Want to go?"

She followed him out to the parking lot where a car, the same color blue as his cruiser and his sailboat, was parked.

"Is this your own car?" Trish asked.

"No, it's my dad's. He's good about letting me use it, though."

He opened the door on the passenger side for her, and she got in. He leaned down and said to her through the open window, "You'll have to give me directions to your house. Believe it or not, I'm terrible with directions on land, and these streets that wind around Sand Lake only make things worse. Every time I'm sure I have the right one, it turns out to be a dead end."

Jonathan walked around to the driver's side and got in. Once he had the car running, Trish gave him careful instructions. They weren't far from the Everetts' house, but the roads did wind around the lake in a crazy pattern. She could see how a person who wasn't used to them could easily get lost.

Soon they were pulling into the Everetts' driveway. "Want to come in?" Trish offered, once Jonathan had put the car in neutral. She hated to let him go just when she was beginning to relax. Besides, it was not quite nine-thirty. She had another half hour before her curfew.

But Jonathan shook his head. "I've got a lot of things to do tonight myself, and I've got an early morning tomorrow. Some other time, though."

She popped the car door open. "OK. I'll see you Wednesday at three, then."

"Wait. I'll walk you to the door."

She put her hand on his arm to stop him. "That's OK. Some other time, though."

They both laughed. Then Trish realized she still had her hand on Jonathan's arm, and she quickly pulled away.

" 'Bye," he said softly.

She said, " 'Bye," and shutting the car door, she turned and ran to the back door.

"Where's Jonathan?" her father asked as soon as Trish stepped in the door.

"He went home," she told him. "I have studying to do, remember?"

"He could have walked you to the door. I always walked a girl to the door after a date." Her father eyed her sternly.

"He offered, but I told him it wasn't necessary. He was in a hurry to get home. Besides, this wasn't a date."

"If it wasn't a date, what was it?" her father pressed.

"Come on, David," Trish's mother said, appearing behind him in the doorway. Mrs. Everett's short blond hair glowed in the hall light, and Trish looked at her mother with a relieved smile.

"The movie you wanted to watch is starting, David, and the popcorn is ready. Want some, Trish?"

Trish said, "Thanks, but I just had an ice-cream cone. I think I'll go upstairs and do some studying."

"OK, it's here if you change your mind," Mrs. Everett said.

Trish nodded. She wanted to hug her mother, but she was afraid if she took the time to do it, her father would start in again. Turning, she bounded up the stairs.

When she got to her room, she thought about calling Mary, but she stopped herself. Mary probably wouldn't be home, anyway. She had probably gone out with Deke after dinner. Besides, Trish wanted to keep the details of what had gone on that night to herself. Not that much of anything had gone on—not yet, anyway! Still, Jonathan seemed so determined to give her racing lessons. That, together with the way he treated her that evening, told her that she must mean something to him.

Trish lay back on her bed and stared up at the pink canopy above her. Smiling as she pictured Jonathan's big grin, she told herself that Wednesday afternoon wasn't far away.

Chapter Six

On Wednesday morning Trish had trouble concentrating on her last test. She couldn't stop thinking about her lesson with Jonathan later that day. She was afraid something awful was going to happen, and terrible possibilities kept popping into her mind. Monday night had seemed magical, almost too magical. Something just had to go wrong.

Not wanting to face her first lesson alone, especially after Jonathan had told her to bring Mary along, Trish had tried to talk Mary into giving up her tennis lesson that afternoon. Besides, Jonathan was probably bringing Paul, and she wouldn't get to be alone with him, anyway. But nothing Trish said could persuade Mary.

Getting home from her exam a little before noon left her with three hours to wait. She decided to change her clothes, but as soon as she would settle on one outfit it seemed all wrong. Trish wanted to look nice, but she wanted to look as if she always looked that way without any effort.

Finally Trish decided she ought to look as though she was a serious sailor. After all, Jonathan seemed pleased that she was committed to sailing. The trouble was, what did a serious sailor wear? Eventually, she thought a girl who loved to sail and eat vanilla ice cream should look healthy—as though she were a girl in a soap ad.

With that in mind, Trish settled on khaki camp shorts and a flowered Hawaiian-print shirt. The outfit would be loose and comfortable, and the yellow and blue flowers on the shirt would emphasize her blond hair and make her tan seem darker.

She was ready at exactly three o'clock. Sauntering casually down to the dock to meet Jonathan, Trish was confident that she was in control of herself and would, therefore, be in control of her situation.

Jonathan sailed up just as Trish stepped from the bottom step to the dock. "Hi, there," he called cheerfully after he had scrambled to the bow of his boat to grab the dock.

The first thing she noticed was that Jonathan was alone. Quickly shifting gears, Trish determined that things were going to go right, and, to ensure that, she decided to flirt with him. Maybe if she gave Jonathan an indication of how she felt about him, he'd feel free to express his feelings more directly.

"Hi," she answered back in a voice that she hoped was seductive. Then Trish batted her eyelashes at him the way she had seen Mary do it a million times.

"What's wrong?" Jonathan asked, a look of concern clouding his perfect features. "Have you got something in your eye?"

Every ounce of blood in her body came rushing to her face. Thinking quickly, Trish said, "Maybe a little piece of sand." She began rubbing her left eye with the back of her hand. Just as quickly as she started rubbing, she stopped, certain she would smear the supposedly smear-proof mascara she had so carefully applied only minutes earlier.

Jonathan jumped onto the dock. "Here, let me take a look." He took her chin in both of his hands, his thumbs resting lightly on her cheeks. Gently he bent her face close to his own.

"I don't see anything," Jonathan assured her after a moment. As he straightened up, Trish found herself wishing that she *did* have sand in her eye—anything to keep him that close! But she knew that was all silly. She decided to stick to being herself and hope for the best.

Seeing that Trish was all right, Jonathan looked at *Lucky Lady* and exclaimed, "Your boat isn't rigged!"

"I didn't know whether to rig it or not. I thought you were bringing Paul. I wasn't quite sure what the plan was." She felt the swarm of butterflies that had been plaguing her lately return.

"I guess I wasn't clear enough," Jonathan agreed, softening his tone. "I thought we could race each other. The wind is about the same as it was the day we played sail tag. How about it?"

His dimpled grin immediately put her at ease. He was the same boy who had played tag with her and who had bought her an ice-cream cone, Trish reminded herself.

Trish nodded enthusiastically. "Sounds good to me."

She looked at the birch trees sticking out along the bank behind them. Their leaves were turning over slightly, but their delicate branches were barely moving. "It doesn't seem too windy. I'm sure I can handle it." She smiled confidently.

"Good. Get your sails, and I'll help you rig your boat," Jonathan offered.

Trish pointed behind her back with her thumb, indicating the boat shed. "I'll be right back." Then she turned and trotted off, afraid that if she were gone too long, Jonathan would disappear.

"Here they are," she panted, tossing the mainsail bag into *Lady*'s cockpit and laying the jib on the dock.

"I've got a good idea." Jonathan's leprechaun eyes twinkled. "Why don't we trade boats for this race? It'll give me a chance to get a feel for your boat and help me give you some pointers that might be relevant to your boat in particular."

She looked at *Lightning*. Its blue deck made it seem especially fierce to her. *Lucky Lady*, though the same class of boat, looked sunny and familiar with her bright yellow deck.

"OK," Trish agreed reluctantly.

"Then you take my boat and start," Jonathan said, scooping up her jib from the dock. "I'll rig your boat and follow you."

Trish watched him jump onto the deck of her boat. Then she asked, "Where are we racing to?"

"Let's go to that channel marker," Jonathan replied, pointing to the buoy they had tied themselves to earlier in the week. When Trish hesitated, he laughed. "Go on," he urged, "or you're going to lose your advantage."

She boarded his boat and took a quick look around. Jonathan had a slightly different setup for his mainsheet, but that was about the only difference between her boat and his. She lifted the painter off the dock post and gave the boat a shove backward with her foot. Then she scrambled to the stern and took hold of the mainsheet and the tiller. The jib, cleated to the mast, would have to take care of itself.

Trish was just beginning to feel comfortable sailing *Lightning*, when she noticed Jonathan shoving off from the dock. When she looked at the sails, she saw that they were both luffing slightly. He was already gaining on her.

Trish pulled the mainsail in tighter and eased the boat downwind. At that point an unexpected puff hurled itself into her, lifting *Lightning* with such force that she had to slip her feet into the hiking straps and lean out over the side of the boat. Clearly, the wind was picking up.

She forced herself to concentrate harder. She didn't care if she lost the race as long as she didn't tip Jonathan's boat over! She could just hear her new nickname, 'Tippy Trish'! Even the thought made her shudder.

Trish came about twice as she tacked to the marker. As she rounded it, she let the mainsail out for the broad reach back to the dock. The wind snuggled into the larger pocket she had created in the sail, and she felt *Lightning*'s flat hull lift to plane across the surface of the water.

As she flew along, she kept expecting Jonathan to pass her. She was so certain that he was right behind her that she didn't let herself look. Her head was pounding, and her heart was racing. Then Trish was landing at the dock, and Jonathan hadn't passed her! She had beaten him!

She turned around to see where he was. Jonathan was close, but she had undeniably won the race. She wanted to scream with joy. She had never dreamed she could beat him, even with a head start. Besides, she gloated, it hadn't really turned out to be all that much of a lead.

"Hey, you!" Jonathan shouted, docking her boat next to his. "You beat me, and with my own boat, too! That's the last head start you get from me!"

She stretched out her long legs and caught

Lucky Lady as she came careening into the dock. She considered saying that she hadn't had all that much of an advantage but decided against it.

"And I thought you needed lessons!" Jonathan said, scoffing and shaking his head and wagging an accusing finger at her teasingly as he stepped from her boat to the dock.

Then a horrible thought struck her. Was this to be both her first *and* her last lesson? "I do need lessons," she insisted. She didn't want him to think she didn't need his help any longer. What if that was the *only* reason Jonathan was there? No, she needed more time with him.

He tilted his head and studied her. "I think you've been teasing me, haven't you? You're really every bit the racer your brother is, aren't you?"

Thinking quickly, she said, "You gave me a head start, remember?"

"Not much of one." He kept looking at her thoughtfully. Then he shook his head. "You're even better than I thought you were. I should apologize for underestimating you. What I'd really like to do now is switch boats and have another go at it, even up this time. But I can't. I have to be at a yacht club meeting in forty minutes. How about Friday?"

"I can't. I promised my mother—" she began.

But he waved the rest of Trish's response away. "You don't need to explain." Jonathan untied his boat, and, before he shoved off, he added, "See you Saturday, then. And remember, I'll have my eye on you." Then he winked and came about.

After he left, Trish watched the triangles of his sails grow smaller and smaller until they finally blended in with the other white triangles on the lake. Then she put *Lady* away and bounded up the stairs to the house to phone Mary. She was relieved to find that Mary was home.

"And that was that," Trish finished after quickly explaining what had happened.

Mary clicked her tongue. "That was a mistake."

"What was?" Trish asked.

"Beating him, you dope," Mary replied.

"I wasn't trying to beat him. I was just sailing. The wind was picking up, and I didn't want to tip his boat over. Do you think I've lost him? Do you think he'll back out of giving me lessons now?" Trish demanded, feeling increasingly desperate. "Everything between us was going so well, too."

"He mentioned Friday, didn't he?"

"I told him I'd made plans. Then he just said he'd see me during the race," Trish answered despondently.

"There you go. It all depends on how you do during the race. If you're rotten, I'm sure Jonathan will offer to go ahead with the lessons," Mary told her.

Trish sighed. "You mean I should do badly on purpose?"

"Got any better ideas?"

"Is that what you'd do if you were able to beat

Deke at tennis?" Trish had a hard time imagining Mary not winning if she could. "Isn't losing on purpose the same as lying?"

Mary laughed. "I could never beat Deke at tennis. He's been playing since he was old enough to hold a racket."

"But you'd beat him if you could. I know you would," Trish insisted.

Without hesitating for a moment, Mary said, "No, I wouldn't. It would damage his fragile male ego. Some things are taboo in this world, you know. Besides, if I did beat him, Deke wouldn't need to give me lessons anymore. Then I wouldn't see him every afternoon.

"But, really, you're worrying too much. What are your chances of beating Jonathan in a real race? After all, he did give you a head start. And it wasn't a real race, anyway. It was just the two of you. No confusion. No crunch."

Trish sighed. "I guess you're right."

"Of course I'm right. Look, Deke's going to be here any minute now. I've got to go."

"Haven't you had your lesson yet?" Trish asked.

"No. He couldn't fit me in until four. I'm still coming over to your house tomorrow, right?"

"I hope so," Trish answered.

"I am," Mary confirmed. "See you then."

" 'Bye," Trish responded. After hanging up the phone, she stretched out on her bed. Trish was still mulling over the day's events when the phone rang.

Expecting it to be Mary calling back for some

last-minute reason, Trish picked up the receiver and drawled a lazy, "Hello?"

"Hi, Trish. It's Jonathan."

"Oh, hi," she said casually as she sat quickly upright, all of her emotions snapping to attention. It was actually him!

"Look. As it turns out, I'm free tomorrow. I don't have to work, after all. Can we schedule a lesson for sometime tomorrow?" he asked.

"Mary's coming over—" Trish began.

"Excellent! What time?" Jonathan asked.

She answered, "Around noon, I think."

"Great. I'll get Paul, and we'll come over around two." Before she could even say goodbye, he'd hung up.

"Why aren't they coming until two o'clock?" Mary demanded, storming into the kitchen and immediately opening the refrigerator. "I thought you said you'd make me lunch. Where's your mother?"

"She's running errands, I guess." Trish watched her friend pull out nearly everything in the refrigerator. "We can make lunch without her. We've done it a million times before."

"That's not what I'm worrying about." Mary seemed to settle on a package of turkey roll, a tomato, and lettuce. She put everything else back. "What I *am* worried about is getting home by four o'clock. I have plans, remember?"

"I remember. You'll be home by then," Trish promised. "Say, leave those pickles out. I'll get the bread. Do you want chips?"

"Of course," Mary replied. "What's a sandwich without potato chips?"

"Sorry, Mary. All we have are *corn* chips."

Mary groaned. "It isn't my day, is it?"

Trish laid out four slices of wheat bread and began doling out the turkey. "Well, you wanted Jonathan to come over again, didn't you?"

"Sure, but I also wanted potato chips, and I definitely want to be home by four o'clock."

Trish covered her heart with her right hand. "I promise you'll be home by four o'clock if I have to ride you there myself on the handlebars of my bicycle," she vowed.

Mary laughed. "Let's just hope it doesn't come to that."

"Come on," Trish ordered, waving her fork at Mary. "Slice up that tomato and deal out those pickles. Everything will fall into place."

"Listen to you!" Mary exclaimed. "Aren't you the picture of confidence."

"Shouldn't I be?" Trish countered.

Mary shrugged. "Sure," she answered absently. "Why not?"

Things with Jonathan had been going well so far, Trish told herself. But then again, if things were as good as they seemed, why hadn't Jonathan asked her out? She was confused. "I don't think I'm very hungry after all. Put those pickles away," she ordered.

"I will not. I'm going to have one even if you're not." Mary began to open the jar. Then she stopped. "You aren't having a crisis of confidence, are you?"

"It's already twelve-thirty," Trish said, glancing nervously at the clock.

Mary shook her head. "This is all my fault. I'm sorry. Look, after we eat, we'll go upstairs and find something special for you to wear, something that will take Jonathan's breath away when he sees you. The right clothes always make *me* feel more confident." Mary began slicing the tomato.

Trish looked down at her clothes. "What's wrong with what I have on?"

Mary looked up from the tomato. "Nothing. But if you're getting nervous, changing your clothes will make you feel in control again. Trust me."

"All right," Trish answered. She put the slices of tomato on top of the turkey.

Mary topped that with lettuce and a second slice of bread. "Eat up," Mary commanded. "Then we'll go upstairs, and I'll show you what I'm talking about."

After eating lunch, they went up to Trish's room to scan her wardrobe. Trish felt that wearing sailing clothes was the best idea, but Mary as usual had other ideas.

"Sure, looking healthy is all right," Mary agreed, rifling through Trish's things. "But healthy is hardly sensational. You want to get Jonathan more interested in you, don't you?"

"Of course I do," Trish confirmed, gazing over Mary's shoulder.

Mary clicked her tongue critically. "I don't

know why I never noticed that most everything you own is either purple or pink."

"I look good in purple and pink," Trish said defensively, glancing into the mirror above her dresser to confirm that she was still a tall, slim blonde with blue eyes and had a complexion a bit on the dark side.

Mary shook her head. "No one looks good in purple and pink," she assured Trish.

"Oh, well," Mary finally sighed, after rejecting Trish's entire wardrobe as garish. "When all else fails, wear your bathing suit."

Of course, Trish thought. *That was it!* She had worn her bathing suit when they played sail tag, and Jonathan had offered to give her free racing lessons! She trotted to the bathroom and got her suit.

"Here it is," Trish said, tossing the suit on the bed.

"Oh, no," Mary groaned. "The stripes are purple!"

"I—" Trish began, but Mary broke in.

"Don't tell me that you look good in purple or I'll scream."

Still shaking her head, Mary said, "Go ahead. Put it on. What we really should have done today was go shopping." Mary wandered over to the window. "Hey, look!" she called. "Isn't that them?"

Trish rushed to the window in time to see Paul tying *Lightning* to the dock. She looked over her shoulder at the clock. It wasn't two yet. In fact, it wasn't even one-thirty!

"They're early," Trish said with horror. She

had wanted to fix her makeup and brush her hair again, to get herself psyched up.

"Relax," Mary ordered. "Take your time. Make them walk up to the house to get us." Mary's face shone. Trish could see that Mary had shifted into her flirtatious mode. Trish had thought that Mary's confidence would make her feel less nervous, but it wasn't working out that way at all.

Trish felt herself beginning to panic when suddenly the doorbell rang. "What should we do?" she gasped, gripping Mary's arm.

Mary pulled her arm away and gave her a funny look. "Answer it, of course."

Trish took a deep breath and exhaled slowly. "Of course. We'll go to the door." Where, Trish wondered, was the girl who had strode so confidently to the dock the day before? Gone. Trish herself had sent her away. After all, that girl had nearly blown it with Jonathan by being too competent, hadn't she?

"Come on," Mary said, taking hold of her hand and pulling her friend forward at a much faster pace than Trish had been managing on her own. "If we go to the door at your speed, they're going to think no one is home and leave. You don't want that, do you?"

Maybe she did, or part of her did at any rate. Trish realized that her tension was compounded by Mary's presence instead of being eased. It was one thing to blow her chances with Jonathan when she was alone with him, but it was quite another to ruin them in front of a critical audience.

"Hi," Jonathan said when Mary yanked the door open. "I was beginning to think you girls weren't here." He turned sideways, and Paul stepped forward. "Mary, this is Paul Anderson."

"Hi, Paul." Trish watched Mary smile and bat her eyelashes as she greeted Jonathan's crew. Mary looked cute when she did it, and no one asked *her* if she had something in her eye!

"Sorry we're early," Jonathan apologized. "Paul has to be home by four, so I thought since you were going to be here at twelve—"

"That's OK. I have to be home at four myself," Mary said. She gave Trish a little poke.

"I'm glad you're a little early," she responded.

"I thought it would be good if Paul and I raced you two today. No head start, though." Jonathan's eyes pierced Trish's with his challenge. "Is that OK with you?"

Jonathan's challenge awakened something in Trish that eased some of her nervousness. She gave her blond mane a toss and nodded.

"You're ready to get beaten then?" Paul asked with a chuckle.

"We're ready if you are," Trish answered a bit too calmly. Mary gave her a little sideways glance that seemed to say, "Don't be dumb. Let them win."

Trish did see her point. But she also felt a little tickle deep inside of herself. Trish knew she wanted to win, or, at the very least, to *try* to win, even a race as small as this one. Besides, how would Jonathan feel if he ever knew Trish had let him win? She knew she didn't want anyone letting *her* win; that would be worse than losing.

"Where to this time?" Trish asked Jonathan as the four of them walked down to the dock.

"The course will have to be a short one." Jonathan looked out at the lake. "I'll think about it while you're getting your boat rigged. There's a decent wind today, isn't there, Paul?"

"Trish knows that," Paul said. "She's all set to tip over. Aren't you, Trish?" he teased. "I mean, you've got your bathing suit on and everything."

Trish felt her face burn. She hadn't thought about what wearing her bathing suit could mean. She looked around and realized that the others were all dressed. Why did she ever let Mary talk her into changing?

"I'll get the sails," Mary offered, already heading for the boat house.

"I'll go with you," said Trish.

Once they were alone in the shed, Mary said, "Don't let that oddball friend of Jonathan's upset you."

Trish took the mainsail bag down from its hook. "Don't worry. Paul's teasing doesn't bother me," she lied.

When they got back on the dock, the boys had *Lady* down from her lift. Jonathan took the sail bag from Trish and tossed it onto the boat.

"Let's do the same course we did yesterday.

There's more wind, so it should go even faster."
Jonathan looked at Trish for approval, and she
nodded.

"Let's get moving then," Mary said impatiently.

Trish climbed aboard the boat, and Mary followed her. They managed to get the boat rigged
in record time. Mary, it seemed, was already
racing, but she was competing against the clock,
not Jonathan and Paul. She was undoubtedly
worried about getting home in time for her date,
Trish decided.

"Ready?" Paul called from *Lightning* once the
girls had their sails up.

"Ready," Trish called back.

"Then go!" Jonathan shouted.

Mary pushed off at the same moment as Paul,
and the race began! Trish felt the wind fill the
sail and knew that she couldn't try to do anything
but win, despite Mary's advice to the contrary.

The boys got to the channel marker a little
before the girls. Trish still felt as if she might
be able to overtake them, and she doubled her
effort to concentrate, scanning the lake for rov-
ing puffs of wind.

"What are you doing?" Mary demanded as
Trish came about. "You aren't thinking of beating them, are you?"

"Get to the high side!" Trish ordered, ignoring her question. The boys were less than a
boat length away! If she was going to pass them,
she was going to have to do it then or the race
would be over.

"Right-of-way!" Trish yelled from her port tack,

as *Lucky Lady* overtook *Lightning*. Jonathan looked astounded as the girls slid by. Trish had a brief moment of regret, but that feeling was quickly replaced by one of pride. She was not only honest, she was also victorious! Trish couldn't help liking herself.

Then, before she could actually finish in first place, the boys overtook them. Jonathan had beaten her, after all. But not by much. And Trish hadn't had a head start!

When they had tied the boat up at the dock and were beginning to unrig *Lucky Lady*, Jonathan came over and said, "You gave us a run for our money. For a while there, I thought you were going to beat us." He gave Trish one of his warm smiles. "That was a great race!"

"Next time—" Trish told Jonathan threateningly.

Jonathan nodded. "Well, we've got to go or I won't have Paul home in time." He seemed reluctant to go.

" 'Bye," Trish said. "I'll see you soon." Then, Jonathan turned around and jogged back to his boat.

"Idiot." Mary sighed, shaking her head.

"What do you mean?" Trish demanded. "He wasn't upset about the race. If anything, he was excited."

"I wasn't talking about the race," Mary told her.

"What *are* you talking about, then?"

"You should have asked Jonathan to come

107

back after he dropped off Paul. I'd be gone by then, and the two of you could have been alone."

Mary shook her head as she yanked the long wooden batons from the Dacron sail. "Racing lessons aren't the only lessons you could use," she added, wagging a baton at Trish.

"And you're the one to give them to me?" Trish asked playfully.

Mary laughed. "Actually," she said as she rolled the jib sail around its little wooden boom, "you're doing all right with Jonathan, Trish. In fact, I'd say you had him in the bag."

Chapter Seven

"Hey! Good job!" Mary cried as the girls sailed across the finish line about midfleet at Saturday's race.

It wasn't winning, but Trish was happy. It was the best they had done so far. "Good job, yourself."

Mary saluted her. "Thanks, captain. I deserve that."

"You do," Trish agreed. "But I thought you wanted to lose."

"Are you kidding? Do you think I was running myself ragged out there so we would lose? I just thought you shouldn't beat Jonathan the other day. I never said anything about not beating the other twenty-three boats in the fleet."

Trish nodded. "Well, a skipper is only as good as her crew."

"True," Mary agreed. "So very true."

Trish nodded again, and they both laughed.

Trish felt good about the start they had had and their ability to hold on to the place throughout the race. She felt so good that she wanted to celebrate.

"Let's stop off at the yacht club," she suggested.

"OK," said Mary. "I don't have to be home at any particular time since I'm not seeing Deke tonight."

Trish raised her eyebrows as she let the sail out. "You're not? How come?"

"There's a tennis tournament at the club, and he's sort of responsible for making sure everyone involved has a good time. He'll be tied up practically twenty-four hours a day until the whole thing is over."

"I've got a good idea. As long as you're not going out with Deke tonight, why don't you stay over at my house? You'll just have to come back in the morning for the next race anyway," Trish reasoned.

"Great! Oh, Trish, it's been ages since I spent the night at your house. We could even paint our toenails some outrageous color or something," Mary said eagerly.

"It's settled then," Trish said, just as they reached the yacht club dock. She turned the boat into the wind, and Mary tied *Lady* onto the back of another boat.

"Hi, Trish," a couple of other kids called to her as she and Mary were letting the sails down.

Trish waved to them, but ninety percent of her attention was devoted to looking for Jonathan. "Could you tell who won the race?" she asked Mary.

Mary shook her head. "I was too busy watching all the action around us. Racing in a crowd as big as that is entirely different from straggling along behind the fleet, isn't it?"

"Hi, there, you two," someone on the dock said.

Turning to see who it was, Trish thought it might be Jonathan. But it wasn't—it was Paul. Looking past Paul, she saw Jonathan, leaning against the clubhouse, talking to an older man. She wanted to rush over to him, but he looked as though he was in the middle of an important conversation.

"Hi," Paul repeated. "Remember me?"

"Hi, Paul," Mary greeted him.

Without asking if it was all right, he stepped across the other boat and boarded *Lucky Lady*. "How did you girls do today? I see you're dry, so I assume you stayed afloat. You didn't sink anyone else, did you?"

"We did all right," Trish told him, not letting his teasing spoil her good mood. Then she asked, "Who's that with Jonathan?"

Paul turned and looked in the direction she was looking. "You don't know?" He sounded incredulous. Trish shook her head. "It's the old man himself, Dick Driscoll."

Trish shrugged. The name meant nothing to her.

"Commodore of the yacht club? You know,

it's similar to being the president of a club," Paul clarified. "Boy, you *are* in the ozone, aren't you, Everett. How can you be a member and not know who your leader is?"

Trish ignored this challenging remark as she had ignored his earlier one. "What do you suppose they're—" she started to ask. But before she could get the entire question out, Mr. Driscoll slapped Jonathan on the back and began walking away. Jonathan looked over in their direction and waved.

"Do I suppose what?" Paul asked.

Trish waved back at Jonathan, and he started walking toward them. "Never mind," she told Paul.

"Hi, girls," Jonathan said as he stepped along the other boat on his way to *Lady*. "How'd it go?"

Trish shrugged modestly. "Better. How about you?"

"We did better than just better, Trish," Mary put in. "We came in somewhere in the middle, I'd guess. We were in the thick of it the whole race." Mary grinned proudly.

"We came in first," Paul told them. "No one was even close to us. We were a one-boat fleet today." Where Mary had sounded proud, Paul sounded smug.

Jonathan shook his head. "Just listen to that guy. He's a one-man fan club. Although, I'm sure we won't be unchallenged for long, Paul. Trish will be giving us a run for our money soon. Right,

Trish?" Jonathan put his hand on her shoulder and gave it a squeeze. Even that brotherly gesture sent shock waves through her sys-tem. She imagined herself slipping her arm around his waist and giving him a squeeze in return.

"Come on," Jonathan said, taking his hand away. "Let's all go up to the clubhouse. I'll treat everyone to a victory soda."

"I've got a better idea," Paul interjected before anyone could make a move. "Why don't the four of us go out for a pizza later?"

"Great idea!" Mary cried eagerly. "I'm sleeping over at Trish's house tonight, so you guys could pick us both up there. How about it, Trish?"

Trish looked at Jonathan to see if he was as eager about Paul's plan as Paul was. She'd put up with Paul to be with Jonathan. But she wasn't sure she could stand a whole evening with Paul if Jonathan wasn't going to be there.

"I could go for pizza," Jonathan said, much to Trish's relief. "What time should we pick you girls up? It should be an early one. We're all racing tomorrow, right?"

"How about seven o'clock?" Trish suggested.

After that was settled, Jonathan and Paul scrambled onto the other boat and cast the girls off.

"I hope I'm not getting you into trouble," Trish told Mary after they were a safe distance from the island.

"Oh, no. I'm sure my parents won't mind if I stay at your house," Mary assured Trish.

"I wasn't thinking of your parents. I was thinking of Deke. How will he feel when he finds out that you went out for pizza with another guy?"

"Don't worry. He's much too secure to be jealous. Besides, I've told him all about you and Jonathan," Mary said.

"You what?" Trish shouted, nearly dropping the tiller.

Mary smiled sheepishly. "We tell each other everything."

"About me?"

"About everything," Mary replied with a shrug.

"Please remind me of that the next time I start to tell you anything, will you? Coming about," Trish added, quickly giving the tiller a shove and leaving Mary barely enough time to duck her head.

"Pizza, huh?" Mrs. Everett said after they had called Mary's parents and gotten the go ahead on the evening. "Are you sure that's going to be enough supper for you girls after racing all afternoon?"

"If it isn't, they can always have something when they get home, Barbara," Mr. Everett assured his wife. "By eleven o'clock, right girls?"

Mary and Trish nodded in unison even though Trish knew Jonathan would probably have them home long before that. He'd said early, and she was sure he'd meant something more around ten o'clock and possibly even earlier. Racing was much more important to Jonathan than a night out.

"You could have something to eat now, before you go," Mrs. Everett suggested. "I've got some lovely slices of roast beef in the fridge. I'd be more than happy to make each of you a nice sandwich."

"Not for me," Mary answered. "But thanks anyway, Mrs. E."

"Me either, Mom. Thanks." Trish started backing out of the living room toward the stairs. "Come on, Mary. Let's go up to my room." It was getting close to seven, and Trish hadn't even begun getting ready.

"What should I wear?" Trish wailed once they were safely behind the closed door of her room. She had vowed never to ask Mary that question again but was finding that vow impossible to keep as her anxiety level increased.

"I don't know. A better question is, what am *I* going to wear? I don't have anything here but what I've been wearing all day. I didn't even think of that until now." Mary eyed herself critically in the mirror above Trish's dresser.

"You look fine," Trish assured her. "You always look terrific. I'm the one that needs help."

Mary turned away from the mirror and confronted Trish. "You know, the fair thing to do would be for both of us to go as is."

"What's fair about that? I'm trying to make an impression, remember? Look, you can borrow something of mine," Trish offered.

Mary turned back to the mirror and examined her ample chest. "Thanks but no thanks.

115

I'd rather be sweaty than bursting out of one of your blouses."

"Thanks!" Trish cried indignantly. "I'm not *that* flat chested."

"I didn't say you were. It's just that I'm so—"

Mary was interrupted by the doorbell.

Trish gasped. "It must be them!"

"Keep cool," Mary advised her. "You've got time to change your blouse." She pulled a light purple print from Trish's closet. "Here. Put this on with a pair of white jeans."

"I thought you hated purple," Trish said, taking the blouse from her.

Mary winked. "On me. On you, it looks great. Where's your makeup? At least I can use some of that."

When they got downstairs, the boys were sitting in the living room talking to Mr. Everett, or rather, Jonathan was talking to him. Paul was staring out the window at the lake.

"Here they are at last," Trish's father said, noticing them first.

Jonathan sprang to his feet. "Hi, girls. All set?"

"You bet we are," Mary answered pleasantly.

Paul rose a little more slowly than Jonathan had and joined the group. "I know I'm ready. I'm so hungry I feel faint."

Trish's mother joined her father. "Hello, Jonathan and Paul," Mrs. Everett said after Trish had introduced them. "I've been hearing so much about you both lately."

Trish had no idea what her mother meant. She had told her parents that Jonathan was giving her lessons and that he had a terrific sailing history, but she hadn't said anything more than that. She hadn't told them she liked Jonathan in any special way and hoped he shared her feelings. Trish couldn't remember mentioning Paul to them at all.

Feeling eager to hasten their departure before either one of her parents could say anything else to cause her more embarrassment, she glanced at the ship's clock on the mantelpiece and said, "It's nearly seven-thirty already. We should be going." Everyone agreed to that, and they were on their way.

When they got to the car, Mary quickly hopped into the backseat. Jonathan opened the front door for Trish, while Paul got in the back with Mary. *So far so good,* Trish told herself.

At the pizza parlor, Mary and Trish found an empty booth while the boys went to the counter to order the pizzas.

While they were gone, Mary asked, "How am I doing? Am I helping?"

Trish nodded. "But don't go overboard. You don't want Paul to think you're interested in him, do you?"

"If he thinks that, he's more of an oddball than I thought," Mary said, laughing.

The boys came back to wait for the pizza, and the conversation naturally drifted to sailing. Paul complained a little about always being someone

117

else's crew. Trish sympathized with him, and Jonathan even offered to let him skip a race or two during the summer.

Paul only laughed. "Sure. And wreck *Lightning*'s record. You've got to have your own boat and sail all the time in order to be really good. You're lucky," he added, indicating both Trish and Jonathan who were sitting side by side in the booth across from Paul and Mary.

Trish knew what he meant. Until then, she had always assumed she wasn't as good as Clark. Now she knew she had never been given the chance to see what she could actually do. In just a few short weeks she could feel her sea legs getting stronger right along with her desire to win.

As the conversation turned to how Mary felt about racing, Jonathan's name was called, and the boys went to pick up the pizzas at the window. Trish was busy watching Jonathan when she heard Mary squeal.

"What's wrong?" Trish asked.

Mary pointed. "Look who just walked in!"

Trish followed Mary's finger and saw Deke, surrounded by what seemed to be a horde of girls. "Good grief. He looks as though he's a sheikh out with his harem. Is that part of the tennis tournament?"

"I don't know. Don't look at him. Maybe he won't see us," Mary said, ducking her head behind the napkin in despair.

But before Trish could look away, Deke spotted them. "Mary!" he cried and, after saying something to the crowd around him, he started over to their table. When Deke reached them, he slipped into the booth next to Mary.

"Hi, Trish," Deke said, draping his arm possessively across Mary's shoulders and giving her a squeeze.

"Hi, Deke," Trish responded, as always impressed by Deke's easy manner. He was dressed in tennis whites that emphasized his dark hair and eyes as well as his perfect tennis tan. Deke and Mary made a very handsome couple indeed, Trish told herself.

"I didn't expect to see you here," Deke said to Mary. "This is a real treat." Impulsively he kissed her cheek. Mary's already rosy cheeks darkened with a pleased blush.

"Now, Deke. Not in public. What will your harem think?" Mary teased.

Deke looked over at the group, which Trish could now see also contained a few boys. "Let them eat pizza," he replied. "Seriously, that's why we're here. That group turned their noses up at the country club food, believe it or not, and demanded that I take them somewhere for a decent meal. According to them, that meant pizza. So, here we are." He gave Mary another squeeze and said, "And now I'm glad. Say, why are you two here, anyway?"

Before either of them could answer, Paul and Jonathan returned, each carrying an extra large pizza. "Hi," Trish greeted them.

Deke started to get to his feet. "Looks like I'm intruding," he said.

"Not at all," Jonathan told him. "I'm Jonathan Stewart," he added, setting the pizza down and extending his hand for Deke to shake.

"Oh," Deke said, shaking Jonathan's hand. He appeared to be relieved. "I've been hearing a lot about you lately, Jonathan. I'm Deke McDonald."

"And this," Jonathan said, indicating Paul, "is my friend Paul Anderson."

"Paul crews for Jonathan, just as I crew for Trish," Mary added quickly, pulling Deke back down next to her in the booth.

"Nice to meet you both. Well, I better get back to my group," Deke said without moving.

"Why don't you join us?" Jonathan offered. "We've got more than enough pizza."

Deke looked at Mary. Clearly, Mary's twinkling blue eyes were saying yes. "Well, just for a few minutes. I have an obligation to make sure my group's having a good time."

Jonathan sat down next to Trish, and Paul, left with no choice, pulled a chair over to the booth from the table behind them.

"So, you're a tennis player," Jonathan said as he took a slice of the nearest pie.

Deke nodded and then shook his head, declining the slice of pizza Mary was offering him. "And a tennis teacher for this summer. I got the job I've always wanted—assistant pro at the tennis club. I get to do what I love best, next to being with Mary, of course, and get payed for it, too."

Jonathan nodded. "I know what you mean. I teach sailing and love it."

"Trish is Jonathan's student," Mary put in.

"Not his only student, though," Paul nodded. "He also teaches at the yacht club."

"You do?" Trish asked with surprise.

"That's my morning job. I thought you knew, Trish. Anyway, it's nothing new for me. I taught children's sailing class on Lake Linda last summer for the Minneapolis Park Board. Teaching racing lessons is new for me, though, and it's been a real challenge. I find I'm having to think out all my actions stey-by-step. I've been racing for so long I'm barely aware of the things I do while I race," Jonathan explained.

"I know what you mean," Deke said, finally giving in and taking a slice of pizza from Mary. "There's a definite benefit to teaching I never expected. You really learn a lot when you break the process down into individual components, don't you?"

Jonathan nodded appreciatively. Then, glancing around the table quickly, he said, "We forgot to get drinks, Paul. What does everyone want?"

"I'll go get whatever you want," Paul offered, getting up. "I'm kind of a fifth wheel here anyway."

"Get a pitcher of soda, OK?" Jonathan said, handing Paul a five-dollar bill. Paul took the money and walked slowly back to the counter.

"Say, I hope I'm not horning in here or anything. When I saw the girls, I assumed for some reason that they were alone," said Deke.

Mary spoke up. "We were. I mean we are. We're together, but as separate people." She paused, looking as confused by her own words as everyone else appeared to be. "Right?"

"Right," Jonathan agreed quickly. "Just four friends having pizza to celebrate a good race. We're glad to have you join us, Deke."

Trish saw Deke relax and could imagine the four of them out together, having a wonderful time. Jonathan was the kind of boy that put everyone at ease. Perhaps that was how he managed to get along with Paul as well as he did.

Paul came back with a tray containing a pitcher of soda and glasses. Deke stood up before he reached the table. "As much as I'd like to stay with all of you, I've got to get back to my group. Let's do this again sometime," he said to Jonathan.

"Great. I'd like that," Jonathan told him. Then he looked at Trish and smiled.

"Nice meeting you, Paul," Deke said to Paul when he reached the booth.

"Nice meeting you, too," Paul said as he slid into the place next to Mary that Deke had just vacated.

They were down to just half of one pizza as Paul poured the soda. "It's a shame your friend had to go so soon, Mary. I even got another glass for him."

"I think Deke got your hint," Trish told Paul, unable to keep quiet any longer. "You know, the one about being a fifth wheel?"

Paul chuckled. "That *was* a good one." He handed Mary a glass. "Well, is that guy your boyfriend or what?" he asked Mary.

Mary took a sip of her soda and followed that with a bite of her pizza. "Yes," she answered finally. "Deke is my boyfriend."

"He seems to be a nice guy," Jonathan commented. "I'm looking forward to seeing him again. Maybe we could all play tennis together sometime. I'm not very good, but I enjoy playing."

"I didn't know there was anything you weren't good at," Paul said.

"I guess you don't know everything about me then," Jonathan replied, and then he yawned. "I'd like to be home by ten so I'm not tired for the race tomorrow," he added.

Paul shrugged and downed the last of the soda, but he didn't argue. Instead, he said, "Girls? Are you anxious to get home?"

"I'm tired myself," said Trish.

Jonathan smiled at her. "Then it's settled. We're on our way."

This time there seemed to be no question about where anyone would sit. Jonathan opened the door for Trish to sit up front with him, while Paul, followed by Mary, climbed into the back.

When they pulled into Trish's driveway, Jonathan turned off the engine. "If no one objects,

I'd like to take a quick walk to the dock with Trish," Jonathan said.

"I'll wait right here for you," Paul said. "The mosquitos are fierce at this time of the night."

Trish glanced back at Mary. "I'll meet you inside," Mary said, opening her own door and quickly climbing out. Mary was already going into the house as Jonathan helped Trish out of the car.

"Be back in a little bit," he told Paul.

Soon, Jonathan and Trish were strolling across the lawn together in the moonlight. Trish's breath caught in her throat. It seemed as if things were finally going to get started between them.

"Hello," he said softly, taking hold of her hand.

"Hello," she responded shyly, giving his hand a slight squeeze. He returned the pressure, and she felt as if there were a rocket about to be launched in her chest. Trish knew that she couldn't be luckier; she was with the sweetest boy she had ever met.

They started down the narrow stairs to the dock side by side, her hip brushing against his. She felt so light-headed that, even though these were the same stairs she'd climbed at least a million times before, her feet moved awkwardly, as uncertain of themselves as the rest of her was. Every once in a while she stole a quick glance at Jonathan, amazed that a boy so nice also could be so handsome.

"I've been wanting to talk to you all evening," Jonathan said. "But being in a group makes private conversation impossible."

Her heart started beating even faster. He seemed to be on the verge of making some sort of personal confession to her. Trish wanted to make it easier for him. "I know what you mean," was all she could think of to say, though.

Trish felt his eyes searching her out. She lifted her face and swore that she could see the green of those eyes despite the darkness. For a few seconds they looked silently at each other. Then he cleared his throat and said huskily, "I wanted to talk to you about your start today."

He sounded so earnest, so confidential, that Trish didn't know what he was talking about for a moment. Then she realized that he was referring to the way she had started the *sailboat* race!

Trish felt as though she had just been doused with water. Quickly, before Jonathan could see the effect of his words, she turned her head and looked out at the path the moon was creating on the lake. She couldn't let Jonathan see her disappointment.

"I saw you off to the side of the starting line as the five-minute gun went off," he continued, running his hand through his thick hair. "That wasn't a good position at all."

The moon's trail on the water shimmered, and the air was heavy with the scent of summer. Water lapped rhythmically at the wooden planks of the dock. It was so romantic, Trish told herself. What was wrong with him, anyway? Or worse, what was wrong with her?

She longed to say, "Forget sailing and kiss me." But, of course, she couldn't. Trish cared so much for him, from the top of his sandy-haired head to the ends of his sneakered feet, while Jonathan apparently cared only for sailing.

"You know," he went on, waving his hands for emphasis, "I was amazed that you finished as well as you did today. You're a darn good sailor, Trish. I think your major problem is on the starting line."

He spoke as if he were giving her the key to the universe instead of telling her the weak points of her racing technique. Trish could hear his excitement increase in direct proportion to her own disappointment.

"Maybe you're right," she finally agreed, wishing he would at least pick up the hand he dropped when he had started speaking to her. A little breeze struck her abandoned hand, which was still slightly damp. She tucked both hands into the pockets of her white jeans. Taking a deep breath, she inhaled the familiar, comforting smell of the summer evening.

"You know what I think?" Jonathan asked, and she closed her eyes, hoping that he'd finally get personal. "I think we should work on racing starts for a while. What do you think?"

Jonathan was throwing Trish the ball. What did she think? Was he crazy?

She felt as though someone had stuck her with a pin. She was certain that nothing would ever be this perfect again. The magic moment had slipped away and was gone. She wanted to disappear. "Sounds fine," Trish said instead, doing her best to muster some enthusiasm into her voice.

"Good." He sounded relieved. "Well, we better go. Mary's probably wondering where you are, and Paul's probably about ready to steal my car," he joked.

"Probably," she agreed dryly, trying to think of a reason to hold him back, to give him another chance to say something romantic. But she couldn't think of a thing. Her mind was painfully blank.

This time, Jonathan didn't take her hand. Instead, he started up the stairs ahead of her. Trish trailed after him, and up they went, single file.

When they reached the back of the house, Jonathan said, "Good luck tomorrow. Remember to concentrate on that starting-line strategy. I'm willing to bet it'll make all the difference."

Trish took a step toward him. "Thanks, and thanks for the pizza, too," she said, waiting for Jonathan to make the next move toward a goodnight kiss. At that point, she decided, she'd be happy with a peck on the cheek, or at the very least, a squeeze of her hand. All Trish really wanted now was some indication that Jonathan felt something special for her.

Instead, he took a step backward. "My pleasure." Was it her imagination, or did he sound nervous? "See you tomorrow," he added.

She said " 'Bye" and lifted her hand in a half-hearted wave. He walked away and disappeared around the corner of the house.

She listened to his car pulling out of the driveway and finally went into the house. What, Trish asked herself, as the screen door to the porch banged shut behind her, had happened? It had almost been as if Jonathan were suddenly afraid of her. But why? Trish hadn't said or done anything—or had she?

Chapter Eight

"So, what did he want?" Mary asked when Trish got up to her room. Mary had already borrowed a nightgown and was waiting comfortably for her.

"Nothing," Trish answered glumly. She threw herself into her desk chair and sighed.

"Jonathan dragged you down to the lake to tell you nothing?"

Trish got up and sat down on the bed next to Mary. "He wanted to tell me that my problem was bad starts."

"What?"

"Jonathan wanted to talk to me about sailing, about racing starts." Trish rolled over on her back and sighed again.

"And for that you had to be alone?" Mary's tone was incredulous.

"Apparently. Strange, huh?"

"Very strange," Mary agreed.

However, Sunday's race was anything but strange. Just as Jonathan had predicted, Trish did no better in the race than the position in which she had managed to start. She had tried to concentrate on *Lady*'s starting-line position but found she was distracted by all the noise and confusion. All Trish could think about, as all twenty-five of the boats in their fleet clustered around the judges' boat, was not hitting anyone.

"We're on a roll," Mary told Trish as they crossed the finish line. "That's two races in a row that we haven't been dead last."

Trish just couldn't seem to share Mary's enthusiasm. She was now convinced she could do much better if she could cure herself of her starting-line phobia. But how was she going to do that, Trish asked herself? She couldn't get this kind of practice with Jonathan. It was impossible to simulate the start of a real race in a fleet of twenty-five boats.

What she should really do, she told herself, was forget about Jonathan's lessons. Trish needed to race in a smaller fleet about the size of the one on little Lake Linda, until she got her racing legs. But Trish was only fifteen. She could never manage the commute. There didn't seem to be a strategy to solve this problem.

When Mary and Trish got back to the Everetts' after the race, Mary announced that she had decided to go to the club and watch Deke's tournament.

"He was so cute at the pizza parlor," she told Trish. "I really miss him."

Trish and her father drove Mary home. At the Bailys', Mary said, "Come with me, Trish. I'll get you a ride home later."

"No, thanks. I've got some things to sort out," Trish told her friend.

"So, what's the trouble?" Mr. Everett asked as they backed out of the Bailys' driveway.

"Trouble?" Trish repeated. "Who ever said there was any trouble?"

"You did tell Mary you had things to sort out, didn't you?" Mr. Everett paused at the foot of the driveway to wait for a car to pass. He took the opportunity to look directly at Trish with blue eyes similar to her own.

"It's no big deal, Dad," she assured him. "It's just that I seem to be hung up on the starting line. I can't get a good position. Everything happens so fast that I—"

"I know what you mean. I used to feel the same way when I started racing."

"You did?" Trish was astounded. She'd never suspected that anything ever bothered her father. "But you've got a slew of trophies in the den," she protested.

He shrugged. "I got over my confusion. It just takes time. That, and some hard work. I've got a couple of books at home I'll dig out for you that outline some different strategies. Sometimes, having a plan can make you forget the noise and confusion."

Trish settled back in her seat, feeling better.

Now all she had to worry about was time. Trish only had seven weeks left to prove herself. If she didn't do so by then, *Lucky Lady* reverted back to Clark. "It just takes time," her father had said. She hoped seven weeks would be time enough.

On Tuesday evening Trish was poring over the second of the four sailing books her father had given her. The first one had been interesting, but, she decided, not too helpful. The second one didn't seem to be much better. Trish was afraid she wasn't going to find the answers she needed in books. She was beginning to believe she was never going to find a cure for starting-line phobia.

She turned her thoughts to her other immediate problem: Jonathan.

Trish hadn't talked to him since he had left her house on Saturday night. If she had, she might have told him to forget the lessons. But she knew she'd never be the one to call them off, not so long as it meant seeing him. Trish was convinced that Jonathan felt more for her than concern over her racing starts, and she just knew he'd tell her in time. Trish was going to have to be patient, no matter how hard that would be, even though he had had the perfect opportunity Saturday night on the dock. What had stopped him?

She was just cracking open her tenth peanut when the telephone rang. Since most of the rest of her friends had gone away for the summer and Trish knew Mary was at the club with Deke, that left only one person—if it was for her.

"Hello?" she answered tentatively, hoping that the caller was Jonathan.

"Hi, Trish. It's me," she heard the voice she had longed to hear say.

"Congratulations on another first place," she told him.

"Thanks. I heard you came in fifteenth."

"Something like that," Trish agreed. "See, you were right. My race does fall apart on the starting line."

"I'm your teacher, remember? It's my job to know your style better than you do yourself."

His voice was so warm and caring that she hoped Jonathan was talking about more than just her racing style. Then he added, "And that's why I'm calling. I want to talk about our racing lessons."

Trish told herself not to be disappointed, but she was, anyway. Mary had been right about strategy. It was a necessity, both on and off the boat. If only Trish had a good strategy for diverting Jonathan's attention from racing to her.

"So, when's our next lesson?" she asked. "I've been doing a little reading, and I'm anxious to try a few things out."

He chuckled. "I like your attitude, Trish. How about tomorrow? I have to teach my class in the morning, but if you sail out to the island about noon, we can probably use some of the yacht club stuff to set up a mock starting line."

"Can you duplicate the noise and confusion?" Trish kidded.

"Sorry, no. I can only give you some strategies to use in different situations. We won't even sail; we'll use those little magnetic boats they have at the yacht club for protest hearings. I think if you have some specific ideas in your head, you won't even notice the mayhem at the starting line anymore."

"All right, I'm willing to give it a try. It certainly can't hurt." Then she had a brilliant idea. "Why don't I come early?" she suggested. "I could watch your teaching technique with the younger set."

"That's fine with me," he answered. "Class starts at ten-thirty."

"See you then," Trish promised.

"I'll be looking for you," Jonathan told her. "I don't suppose you could entice Mary to join us."

"I'm afraid not." She didn't add that Mary couldn't join them because Trish had no intention of asking her. Riding with Jonathan by herself would give her a chance to work on her strategy for winning him.

"Paul will be around, I think. I'm sure he'd be willing to help us out if we need him. I know he comes on a little strong at times, but he's a good guy at heart."

"He must be a good crew," Trish responded.

"He is. I wouldn't be doing as well as I've been doing without Paul," Jonathan assured her. "He's reliable and punctual besides knowing his way around a boat. I was lucky to get him to crew for me this summer."

And Paul was lucky to have Jonathan ask him to crew for him, Trish thought. Jonathan was so loyal, so patient. If only she could be as lucky as Paul.

On Wednesday morning Trish meant to start out to the island by nine-thirty so she wouldn't miss Jonathan's class. But before she could get out of the house, her mother insisted that she change the sheets on her bed and clean her bathroom.

By the time she finished those chores, it was nearly ten o'clock. Since she knew they probably wouldn't be sailing during her lesson anyway, she decided to take the motorboat over to save time.

Unfortunately, the motorboat was no time saver. Whoever had used it last, quite possibly Trish herself, had left the gas tank empty. Struggling with the gas can and priming device cost her even more precious time than her mother had.

Trish finally got to the island at a quarter to eleven. As she drew up to the dock, she saw Jonathan and his fleet of dinghies out in the middle of the bay. She considered motoring out to them but decided that such a move would disrupt Jonathan's teaching. She'd just have to watch him conduct his class from the island.

Trish steered the boat up to the nearest of the three docks, and after tying it up, she turned off the motor. She looked around and saw Jonathan's blue cruiser. Trish also spotted another motorboat she didn't recognize. Then she remembered that Paul might be around. Trish knew he didn't have a sailboat of his own, but his family did live on the lake. They undoubtedly owned a motorboat.

She decided to look for Paul. Perhaps he'd be more at ease and less sarcastic if she talked to him alone. She was feeling so good about things in general that she decided it was worth a try. After all, if Jonathan liked Paul, Trish told herself, there had to be something good about him.

When she reached the nearest door to the clubhouse, Trish could hear voices inside. Perhaps the unknown boat wasn't even Paul's. Maybe he wasn't even there yet.

She paused by the soda machine before going inside, and decided to buy a Coke. Digging into her pocket, she searched for change.

"And she has a crush on him a mile wide," Trish heard someone that sounded like Paul say. "She's so obvious, it's comical. You just watch when she gets out here."

Trish didn't want to hear any more. She wished she hadn't heard what was said so far. But she was rooted to the spot. Who was Paul talking to, she wondered? She felt she knew whom he was talking about—Trish herself.

"She thinks he's doing it because he likes her?" another male voice Trish didn't recognize asked.

"Who knows *what* she thinks," Paul said, sniggering. "She's like a puppy dog."

"Guess that's why they call it 'puppy love,' " the other boy put in.

Trish shifted her weight from one foot to the other. She wanted to see who the other boy was, but she didn't want to risk being seen herself. Could they really be talking about her? So far, they hadn't mentioned her by name. Maybe they were talking about some other girl altogether.

"And, get this, her brother put him up to the whole thing," Paul said after a brief pause. "That's the best part of all. Her own brother!"

"That doesn't surprise me," the other boy said. "Haven't I always said that Clark Everett is a vicious competitor? He'd take on his own grandmother if he could swing it. He couldn't keep his fingers out of the yacht club even though he's not here to sail himself. He had to make a bet just to stay in the thick of things . . . and over his own sister, too." She heard him click his tongue.

Trish felt hot tears spring to her eyes. They *were* talking about her! She, unfortunately, was the only sister Clark Everett had. How could Clark use her that way?

"It was more of a dare than a bet, really," Trish heard Paul say as silent tears began running down her cheeks. "Why, he . . ."

But Trish didn't wait for Paul to finish. She took a few careful steps away from the clubhouse door, then began running back to her motorboat.

Trish climbed aboard and lifted the painter from the post on the dock. She gave a mighty shove with her foot. The motorboat drifted backward. She yanked the rope on the engine, and the motor started right up.

Backing the boat up a little farther, she turned it around and threw the engine into forward. As the boat began picking up speed, Trish saw Jonathan leading his dinghy fleet back to the island. Before she could look away, Jonathan waved. Trish could see his sand-colored hair blowing away from his face in the wind, and the sight of it made her broken heart crack a little bit more. And Trish had thought he was kind! Conniving was a better word for it. Looking away, Trish pretended she hadn't seen him. Then, opening the engine up all the way, she sped off.

Trish was up in her room when she heard someone knocking on her door. "Just a minute, Mom," she called.

The door opened and there stood Mary. "It's not your mom; it's me." Mary looked at Trish a second and immediately said, "You look terrible. What's wrong?"

The look on Mary's face didn't help Trish feel any better. Figuring that she looked even worse than she had thought she did, Trish burst into a fresh round of tears.

"Good grief," Mary said. "Nothing could be

that bad." She turned around and closed Trish's door.

Rubbing at her eyes with the soggy piece of tissue she had been clutching, Trish said, "It's worse than bad. It's the worst thing that's ever happened to me in my whole life."

Mary sat down on the edge of Trish's rumpled bed. "Nothing's happened to Clark, has it?"

"Unfortunately, no," Trish snapped.

"Trish!" Mary admonished. "I know you two have had your spats and all. But Clark is your brother and—"

"Not after today." Her chest gave a painful heave. "I'm disowning him."

"What did he do?" Mary demanded. "What *could* he do? He's still in Maine, isn't he?"

"He doesn't have to be here to run my life, or I should really say to *ruin* my life! Do you know what he did?"

"No," Mary replied cautiously.

"He arranged my sailing lessons with Jonathan."

Mary smiled. "Well, that was nice of him."

Trish scowled. "Clark didn't do it to be nice. He made some sort of bet with Jonathan that I was unteachable, I guess. Jonathan isn't helping me because he likes me. He's helping me to prove himself to Clark!" Trish shrieked, all her previous sadness turning into anger.

"All right, all right!" Mary said. "You don't have to shout at me. *I* didn't do anything."

Trish's face tightened as her anger increased. "I've just begun to shout. I'm no patsy they can use to prove themselves. I'm a person, too, you know."

"I know you're a person," Mary assured her. "*I* never said you weren't."

"It's downright dehumanizing, that's what it is!" Trish added, getting to her feet and beginning to pace the length of her room.

"How did you find out about this bet, anyway?" Mary asked.

"I heard about it from Paul," Trish stormed.

"Paul? How come Paul told you?" Mary watched Trish pace. Finally she said, "Sit down, will you? You're harder to follow than a tennis match!"

Trish threw herself into her desk chair. "Paul didn't exactly tell me. I overheard him telling someone else about it."

Mary shook her head. "Let me get this straight. You heard Paul telling someone else that Clark had made a bet with Jonathan, and you didn't even bother to find out from Jonathan whether it's true?"

"I know what I heard is true," Trish insisted. "It makes too much sense *not* to be true. I've found the missing part to the jigsaw puzzle. It certainly explains why Jonathan was so anxious for me to agree to his 'free' lessons."

"So what if it is true?" Mary asked, standing up. This time Mary did the pacing. "Your sailing has gotten better, hasn't it?" Trish nodded. "You've spent time with a gorgeous guy, haven't you?"

"And I've also become the laughingstock of the entire yacht club," Trish added.

"Paul Anderson hardly qualifies as the entire yacht club," Mary retorted.

"No, he's more like a public-address system. If Paul knows, everyone knows or at least they will know before he's finished." Trish sighed. "I wish *I* was the one who'd gone to Maine."

"So, what do you plan to do about it?" Mary asked, sitting back down on Trish's pink-covered canopy bed.

"What can I do?"

"You could pretend you never heard Paul. You could carry on with business as usual," Mary advised.

"Knowing that Paul and who knows how many other people are laughing at me behind my back? You might be able to handle that one, Mary, but I can't." Trish stared thoughtfully out her window at the lake. Then she said, "I could quit racing. That way I wouldn't have to show my face at the club again."

Mary stood up again. "You can't do that!" she cried. "We're getting better and better all the time. We're really a pretty good team, and we're having a good time, aren't we?"

Trish shrugged. "I don't know anymore. Thanks to Clark, my whole summer is tied up with my feelings for Jonathan."

"Look at it this way. If you quit, Clark will win the bet, won't he? And, on top of that, he'll get to finish the racing season when he comes home."

"Maybe that's what this is all about. Clark Everett, the winner, and Trish Everett, the loser," Trish countered.

"Well, don't be too hasty," Mary advised. "You know what they say about cutting off your nose to spite your face." She walked to Trish's bedroom door and opened it.

"Where are you going?" Trish asked.

"Home, I guess. I had my mom drop me off so we could go sailing or something this afternoon, but I can see you're not in the mood to do much of anything."

Trish followed Mary to the door. "How will you get home?" she asked.

"I'll call my mom and see if she's home from the store yet, I guess," Mary answered.

"My mom can probably take you home. Come on." Trish slid past her into the upstairs hallway. "I'll ride along."

After she had dropped Mary off, Trish's mother asked if they'd had a fight.

"Nothing like that, Mom," Trish assured her.

Her mother stopped briefly at the end of the Bailys' driveway. "You seem upset about something, honey. Want to tell me about it?" she asked, her pale blue eyes reflecting concern.

Deciding that it was the perfect time to bring up quitting, Trish launched into a list of reasons why she was discouraged about sailing.

Her mother listened, nodding her head now and then but not interrupting.

When Trish ran out of steam, she stopped, waiting for her mother to try talking her out of quitting. But her mother only sighed and kept driving.

"I have to admit I'm disappointed, Trish," she said finally. "Your father and I have been so proud of the effort you've put into racing, starting with your determination to be given the chance to race the boat in the first place." She tucked a wisp of her blond hair, so similar to Trish's own, back into place as she waited for a traffic light to change to green. When it did, her mother shifted the little silver station wagon into first gear and pulled ahead.

"On the other hand," her mother continued, "I can't force you to go on with something you don't want to do. If you're not having fun, there's no reason to stick with it. It's not as though you have to prove anything to your father and me, you know."

Trish felt herself flinch as her mother hit an exposed nerve. Proving something. That was the whole point, wasn't it? She was trying to prove something to Clark, to her parents, and to herself. Jonathan was trying to prove something to Clark and to all the sailors on Sand Lake. Even Paul was trying to prove something to someone. Where would it all end, Trish asked herself?

"What about Dad?" she finally asked as her mother pulled into their driveway. "He isn't going to let me quit, is he? He'll say quitting isn't the Everett way."

"I'll take care of your dad," her mother said, reaching over to pat Trish's knee. "If this is what you *really* want," she added.

After her mother had parked the car, Trish walked out on the dock to think. It was nearly time for her father to come home from work. If she didn't tell her mother she had changed her mind about quitting before her father got home, her mother would tell her father. Then it would be all over.

She looked at *Lucky Lady* sitting in her lift, and suddenly she knew that quitting wasn't the answer. She turned toward the house and took the stairs two at a time. Trish had to stop her mother before it was too late.

"Trish! Telephone!" her mother called from the bottom of the stairs the next day.

Trish opened her bedroom door. "OK, Mom. Thanks," she called back.

Probably Mary, she told herself. Mary undoubtedly wanted to find out if Trish had told her parents she was giving up racing.

She picked up the receiver and said, "Hi."

"Hi. It's me," Jonathan said, catching her totally off guard. "Where did you run off to yesterday? I tried calling you last night, but no one was home."

Trish knew he had called. Her parents had been out, and she hadn't answered the phone because she knew it would be Jonathan. Trish had thought he would give up, but she should have known better than that. A boy as determined as Jonathan didn't give up anything easily.

"I had to go home. I forgot I had to be somewhere at twelve," she told him lamely.

"I thought you were going to ride in the motorboat with me while I gave my lesson. I waited as long as I could for you, but ten nine-year-olds can be pretty impatient." Jonathan sounded apologetic, and she felt her resolve soften. Trish could almost see his sincere eyes penetrating her own.

"I'm sorry," she said. "My mother made me do a hundred things around the house before she'd let me leave." Suddenly, Trish realized *she* was apologizing to *him* when *he* should be the one apologizing to *her*! Jonathan wasn't sincere, he was calculating. And Trish had almost fallen for his trick again. Her anger returned.

"Paul set up those little metallic boats I mentioned. I even stopped a couple other skippers and got their input. We had a brainstorming session. It was a lot of fun, but it was meant for you, really. I wish you'd been there," Jonathan said. He didn't sound angry, only disappointed. But, of course, he was, she told herself. Jonathan had wanted her there so she'd learn to race well and win his bet for him, not because he cared about her. As far as he was concerned, she was merely a means to an end.

"I even had a surprise for you," he added when she didn't say anything. "But I'm afraid it won't keep until I see you again since I can't see you before Saturday's race. On top of that," he went on, "next week is the Fourth of July and that means an extra race."

He sighed. Then he said, "Darn it, Trish! I just *know* that session would have meant as much to you as it did to me."

Trish still wanted to tell him off, but he was making it harder and harder for her to do so. What was this surprise he said he had for her? Jonathan made it sound like something personal, a gift of some kind. Still, he hadn't said exactly what. His surprise could very well have been a bag of doughnuts or something else just as meaningless. Part of her still wanted to trust him, to deny that what she had heard Paul say could be true. But Trish wasn't about to let that part of herself have free reign. She had to be tough if she wanted to regain her self-respect.

What Trish needed to do was see him. Maybe she would know if Paul's words were true by just looking at Jonathan. If she only had the nerve to confront him with her suspicions and let him explain himself. All she knew for certain was that she'd have to see him soon, before all her anger wore off and she was once again vulnerable to his good looks and charm.

"Are you sure you couldn't work me in tomorrow?" she suggested, surprised at her own boldness. But then Trish wasn't asking to see him for the same reasons anymore. She wasn't trying to get Jonathan to like her; she was trying to decide if she still liked him as much as she thought she had.

"Friday might just work out. If you could get out to the island early, before my class at ten-thirty, we could spend some time talking, anyway. How does that sound?"

She could hear the eagerness in his voice. Of course Jonathan was eager, she told herself. If there really was a bet on, Jonathan's time was running out!

"I'll see you about nine-thirty tomorrow then."

After Trish had hung up the phone, she lay back against her pink-and-white-flowered bolsters. It was only nine o'clock, but she felt as though it were much later. Tomorrow, she told herself, was the day she'd know once and for all. If it turned out that what she had overheard was true, Trish would finish things with Jonathan and move on to dealing with Clark himself.

Chapter Nine

"**M**ary! What are you doing here?" Trish demanded. Mary stood sheepishly in the doorway. Behind her, Trish could see Mr. Baily backing out of the Everetts' driveway.

"My dad brought me," Mary answered. "After you told me what you planned to do this morning, I just had to come over. The more I thought about it, the more I couldn't let you throw the rest of the summer away over what really amounts to a rumor."

Trish continued to block Mary's entrance to the house. "I'm not planning to throw anything away," she insisted. "As I told you last night on the phone, I'm merely going to ask Jonathan—"

"Who is it, honey?" Mrs. Everett asked, coming up behind Trish. "Mary!" she cried. "Come on in, dear. Trish and I were just having some toast and bacon. Won't you have some with us?"

Mary gave Trish a triumphant smile as she slid past her into the house. "That sounds terrific, Mrs. E., if there's enough to go around."

"There's plenty, and I can always make more," Trish's mother assured Mary as she herded the girls into the Everetts' sunny kitchen.

As Trish watched Mary eat, she had the urge to demand that her friend leave. She had undoubtedly come over to try to stop Trish from telling Jonathan off, but Trish wasn't necessarily going to do that. She just wanted to know the truth. Sinking her teeth into her toast, she told herself she shouldn't have told Mary that she was seeing Jonathan at all.

A little before nine, Trish got up. "Glad you stopped over, Mary, but I have to be going now," she said.

"I know." Mary nodded, getting to her feet too. "I'm going with you."

"Isn't that nice of Mary, Trish?" Mrs. Everett commented. "Don't worry about the dishes, you two. I'll take care of them."

When they reached the stairs to the dock, Trish turned around and asked, "Why are you doing this to me?"

"I'm saving you from yourself. That's all," Mary answered.

Trish glared at her friend. "Then maybe I won't go at all."

"You'll go," Mary told her. "Or I'll go alone and tell Jonathan everything I know myself."

"Go home, Mary," Trish ordered, using her best skipper's voice. "This is my affair."

149

"When you asked me to crew for you last March, you made it my affair, too. You may not have noticed, but while you were getting better, I was getting better, too. I like racing. I want to keep on racing. Besides, I like Jonathan. He's a good guy, and I think he deserves a break."

"Whose friend are you, anyway?" Trish demanded.

"Yours. Come on." Mary slid past Trish and started down the stairs to the dock. "I'm about to prove just what a good friend I am."

"We'll take the motorboat," Trish told her when Mary paused on the dock next to *Lady.* "We're not going to sail with Jonathan, we're just going to talk."

Once they were both aboard the boat, Trish started the engine. She still couldn't believe that Mary had shown up when she had, without any warning. How, Trish wondered, was she going to say what she planned to say to Jonathan with Mary there? Trish had been thrown off course, but she was no less angry than she was when she had overhead Paul. If anything, she was angrier. Trish glared at Mary.

"Look," Mary yelled above the noise of the engine. "I'm merely trying to save you from making a big mistake, one you could regret the rest of the summer and maybe even the rest of your life."

Trish looked past Mary at the morning sparkle of the sun on Sand Lake and didn't answer.

"Besides," Mary went on, waving her arms for emphasis, "Jonathan likes you. I can tell. The bet with your brother may have gotten him started helping you, but now he really likes you!" She gave Trish an encouraging smile.

When they reached the yacht club dock, Jonathan was there waiting for Trish.

"Hi, Trish. Hi, Mary," Jonathan said as soon as Trish cut the engine. "I didn't expect to see you, too, Mary."

"Neither did I," Trish assured him.

Mary just smiled her usual bubbly smile. "I couldn't stay away. Sailing has gotten into my blood this summer."

"You're lucky, Trish. A dedicated crew is hard to find," Jonathan said, offering them both a hand up to the dock.

Trish ignored his hand and stepped onto the dock on her own. "That's right," she said. "*Everyone* seems to be watching out for me this summer."

"I didn't mean—" Jonathan began. But Trish kept right on moving in the direction of the clubhouse, not waiting for him to finish. Mary and Jonathan trailed after her.

"Here's the board," Jonathan told them once they were inside the main meeting room where an oversize green metallic board was propped up on a wooden easel.

"I've seen it before," Trish said evenly.

"I just meant—" he started to explain.

But Mary cut in this time. "*I've* never seen it before. It's really—interesting. What are these things?"

"They represent the boats." Jonathan pulled

one of the little triangles off the green board. "This little movable bar represents the mainsail. It's too small to add a jib." He moved the bar back and forth across the little triangle to demonstrate. Then he turned the little boat over. "See. A magnet."

"What's that big white arrow for?" Mary asked.

"It represents the wind," Jonathan answered.

"I thought Paul was supposed to be here to recreate all the clamor and confusion of the starting line," Trish said.

"He *was* here on Wednesday," Jonathan reminded her. "I didn't want to drag him out here again." His eyes flashed green sparks that seemed to add, ". . . for nothing."

"Well, it's ten to ten." Trish pointed to the big clock near the fireplace. "We'd better get started before we run out of time."

Reaching into his shirt pocket, Jonathan produced a small stack of index cards. "My notes," he explained. "I've been doing some reading on starting the race."

For the next forty minutes, Jonathan moved the little magnetic boats around the metal board, explaining various strategies as he went. Trish found it difficult to listen to him. As each minute passed, she became more frustrated. She couldn't talk to him with Mary there, yet Trish wasn't sure she would be able to say what she had to say even if Mary weren't there.

Whenever Jonathan paused in his lecture to ask for comments or questions, it was Mary who spoke up. "Interesting," was what Mary said most often.

"I hope this makes sense," a clearly exasperated Jonathan finally said. The sound of approaching motorboats signaled the end of their session. It was time for Jonathan's class.

Trish stood up. "Oh, yes," she assured him in a cool manner. "I think *everything* makes *perfect* sense." She turned to Mary, who was still sitting on a folding chair looking at the green metal board, white arrow, and little brightly colored boats. "Don't you, Mary?"

Mary nodded. "If you say so," she said, standing up. Mary looked a little exasperated herself.

After thanking him, Trish and Mary walked down to the dock and boarded the Everetts' red motorboat. Jonathan stayed at the clubhouse, where his class of nine-year-old beginning sailors was gathering.

As the girls pulled away from the dock, Mary shook her head and clicked her tongue.

"What's that for?" Trish asked.

"That's for the way you just treated Jonathan. You sounded so nasty," Mary told her, folding her arms across her chest. "I guess I was wrong. It probably would have been easier on Jonathan if you'd just told him off and gotten it over with."

"That's what I tried to tell you. If I'd been alone, I would have confronted him directly. But you had to butt in, forcing me to snipe away at him indirectly."

"Well, I'm sure he got your message or part of

it, at least. Unfortunately, I doubt whether he knows *why* you were sending him that message. I think you really—"

But Trish twisted the handle of the motor to high, drowning out the rest of Mary's words.

When they reached the dock, Mary said, "I'm going home."

"Good," Trish retorted, securing the motorboat to the Everetts' dock with an angry jerk.

Mary started toward the steps. Then she stopped and turned around. "But I'll be back for the race tomorrow," she added.

Trish looked up at her and smiled. "Good," she said again. Then added, " 'Bye."

Mary shook her head but smiled. " 'Bye," she called before starting up the steps to the house.

Trish cranked the boat lift down so that *Lucky Lady* rested on the water. Then she climbed aboard. Digging a sponge out of the plastic bucket under the bow of the boat, she began to sponge off the deck. As she worked, she began to hear snatches of the things Jonathan had been saying about keeping your eyes on the starting line. Trish could even visualize how Jonathan had positioned the brightly colored boat magnets and how he'd set each one's little sail.

What Jonathan had said made sense; it even made sense out of some of the reading her father had given to her. Dipping the sponge into the lake and squeezing the water out, Trish admitted to herself that Jonathan was a good teacher. Whatever else he was, he was a patient, kind, and thorough teacher, a true professional.

On her hands and knees, she climbed up on the rounded bow of the boat, continuing to clean *Lucky Lady*'s yellow deck. The next day before the race, she and Mary would give the bottom of the boat a good scrubbing.

Next, Trish checked the hardware on the base of the mast to make sure everything was tight. Discovering a loose screw, she scrambled back to the small wooden utility box attached to the boat beneath the tiller and got a screwdriver.

As her thoughts took shape, Trish was glad she hadn't been able to confront Jonathan. She, not Clark, was going to finish the season, and she was going to beat Jonathan Stewart before it was over. Maybe it would take awhile. But eventually, Trish told herself, as she twisted another loose screw back into place, she would do it!

"How do you feel?" Mary asked cautiously when she arrived for the afternoon race Saturday.

Trish laughed. "Terrific!" she answered, ushering Mary into the kitchen. "Come on. Let's grab a quick sandwich. Then we'll wash the bottom of the boat."

Mary followed Trish into the kitchen. "But we just washed the bottom of the boat last week," Mary protested.

Trish pulled the bread out of one drawer and a knife out of the other. "And we're going to start washing it every week, maybe even every race," she told her crew. "Would you get the salami and the mustard out of the refrigerator?"

"So you've given up on quitting then," Mary observed, pulling open the refrigerator door.

Trish got a fresh bag of potato chips out of the pantry. "Quit? Me? Are you kidding? I've barely begun to fight. Before I'm finished, we're going to win a race!"

"I'd settle for simply improving some more," Mary said. She set the salami and the jar of mustard next to the four slices of bread.

"I wouldn't," Trish countered, slapping together two sandwiches and adding a hefty pile of chips to each plate.

As they ate, Mary suddenly said, "You're eating! What does that mean?"

"It means I'm hungry."

"But I've never seen you eat before a race," Mary said.

"I'm over that. I need my strength to win," Trish explained, downing the last of her soda. "Let's get moving." She got to her feet and Mary did the same.

The bottom of the boat was washed quickly, but thoroughly. *Lucky Lady* was among the first boats to reach the starting line. *Lightning* was also among the first. Trish returned Jonathan's wave with a curt nod.

As the rest of the fleet continued arriving, Trish found herself translating the entire situation onto the yacht club's green metal board. When the gun sounded, she was up in the front of the fleet. When the race ended, Trish had finished seventh.

"Wow!" Mary cried when they discovered their place. "We're really hot!"

"Not hot enough," Trish assured her.

Looking questioningly at Trish, Mary said, "It's the best we've ever done."

Trish turned the boat about and headed for home. "It's not the best we're going to do, though. Before we're through, we're going to come in first. Eventually we're going to beat Jonathan Stewart!"

"So that's it?" Mary cried as though a light had just gone on. "Revenge!"

Revenge. Trish considered the word. Her plan was to beat Jonathan at his own game using the very knowledge he had given her and a little of her own know-how as well. Trish hoped Mary was right. Perhaps losing to Trish would upset Jonathan enough to *be* a good revenge. She knew that taking the rest of the season away from Clark would be upsetting to him, especially since it would be Clark's fault that she had.

On Sunday, the wind was nearly as strong as it had been the first race of the season. As Mary and Trish struggled to get the sail raised, Mary said, "Don't you think we could use a third person today?"

"Maybe," Trish answered. "But it's too late to find someone now. I'd have to just call a bunch of names in the yacht club directory."

Trish gave the main halyard an extra tug, then cleated the line on the base of the mast. "We can do it," Trish said firmly, believing that they could. "We'll just have to be extra conscious of hiking out as far as we can."

"I'll do my best," Mary told her. "That's all I can promise."

After the sails were up, Mary cast them off. As soon as the wind hit the sails, they were up and off. Mary hiked out as if her life depended on it, and Trish did the same. Trish was prepared not to do as well as she had the day before, but she was determined that they weren't going to go over. If nothing else, *Lucky Lady* was going to finish the race.

The starting line was already crowded, even though they were early. As *Lightning* sailed past, Trish noticed that Jonathan had a third crew. The old panic washed through her. If Jonathan needed a third person aboard, *she* certainly needed a third crew.

Then Jonathan spotted her. He smiled and waved, just as he had Saturday. He looked so boyishly innocent that it infuriated Trish. Just because Jonathan had a third person, Trish told herself, didn't mean *she* had to also. She gave the tiller a shove and told Mary they were coming about.

"I don't suppose you've forgotten about your plans for revenge?" Mary asked as they were ducking under the swinging sail.

"The word *revenge* was your idea," Trish replied.

"Jonathan has a third today," Mary pointed out as the wind grabbed *Lady*'s sails, forcing both girls to hike out as far as they could manage.

"So?" Trish demanded scornfully. "What does he know, anyway?" She noticed a couple of other boats in their class with only two people aboard. If they could get along without a third, so could Trish!

Suddenly the ten-minute gun went off, catching Trish totally off guard. She looked over at Mary and was pleased to see that she had been paying attention.

"Got it!" Mary said, staring at the stopwatch with satisfaction.

Trish came about again and sailed to the top of the starting line. All the boats were out now, but the noise and confusion didn't bother her. She felt as though she were alone, free to choose the exact spot where she wanted to be when the starting gun was fired.

Once again Trish imagined the metal board, the white arrow, and the little metal boats. It wasn't until Mary started the final countdown to the start of the race that Trish began to worry that another boat would be after her spot, and she suspected that the other boat would be Jonathan's. But, as Mary counted down the last seconds, the place was Trish's! Had she miscalculated? She couldn't help wondering. Was there a better place to be? Trish started to scan the line for Jonathan's boat but had to abandon her search or risk a collision.

Then the starting gun sounded, and they were roaring across the line along with everyone else. Mary manned the back stays and the boards, while keeping control of the jib. The strength of the wind forced Mary to move quickly to accomplish her many tasks, but she handled them all well. By the time they were halfway to the first buoy, it was clear that Trish hadn't miscalculated. They were right up there with the first three boats—with Jonathan himself!

Could they hold that position? They'd been able to hold their starting position in the last race, but that day was different. There was a three-person wind, and there were only two of them in the boat. If she wanted to keep *Lady* where she was, Trish was going to have to take risks. She was ready, and she could tell that Mary was, too.

"Coming about!" Trish yelled, shoving the fully extended dogleg of the tiller toward the sail with all her might. Both girls flung themselves across the boat. They lost no speed in the maneuver!

Trish noticed that one of the other boats with only two people aboard had capsized. She only let that distract her for a second, though.

When they reached the first buoy, they were on the inside of the other two leading boats, one of which was *Lightning*. Trish didn't even look at Jonathan as she held to her inside tack. She could guess his strategy. Jonathan would try to force her to touch the buoy without first declaring that she had the right-of-way.

"Right-of-way!" Trish yelled. Jonathan had to

fall off to avoid the collision, taking the third boat with him. *Lucky Lady* took the lead!

Trish and Mary completed the first lap holding on to the front-running position. It wasn't until they were running toward the last mark of their second lap that a squall caught them and nearly flipped them over, something that never would have happened if a third person had been aboard. In the mad scramble to stay upright, Trish let go of the mainsheet, and the mainsail flapped wildly. That was all Jonathan needed to overtake her.

Now they only had one lap of the course left. She was beginning to feel that if she didn't beat Jonathan that day, she never would. There was a knot of determination in her stomach, and Trish felt lucky. Jonathan wasn't so far ahead of them that overtaking him was impossible, she told herself. She may have lost the lead because of too little weight, but a lighter boat was also an advantage in that it was capable of moving faster.

Then Trish noticed that another boat with only two people aboard had gone over. This time, Mary saw it too. Would she fall apart, Trish wondered? There was no doubt in Trish's mind that Mary was terrified of capsizing.

"Don't look, Trish," Mary told her. "Just because *they* went over, doesn't mean *we* will."

Bolstered by Mary's confidence in her, Trish decided to risk losing her second-place position in order to try for first. "Coming about," she told Mary, switching the tack that had been the mirror of the one Jonathan was taking.

Her move turned out to be the right one. A puff reached her that didn't make it to Jonathan. At the next mark *Lucky Lady* and *Lightning* were neck and neck.

"Right-of-way!" Jonathan yelled. But Trish knew she wasn't close enough to him for there to be any actual threat of collison. He was only trying to intimidate her.

"You've got all the room you need, Stewart," Trish yelled back at him. "And I'm not giving you any more." Then because she was in a position to steal his wind, she did. Gracefully, she moved away from him, into first place.

When the gun sounded, proclaiming Mary and Trish the winners, Trish had to pinch herself to make certain that she wasn't dreaming. All the way to the yacht club, she kept telling Mary that she didn't believe it.

They were lounging against the soda machine, splitting a soda, when a gang of kids from their fleet grabbed them. Carrying both girls back to the dock where *Lady* was tied, they flung them into the water for the ritual, first-win dunking that Trish had completely forgotten about.

As Trish rose to the surface of the water, sputtering for air, she finally believed it. She could see the smiling faces of the other kids; she could hear their enthusiastic cheers. Trish and Mary had actually won! And, what was more, she had beaten Jonathan Stewart!

Trish climbed up on the dock only to be

thrown in again amid more enthusiastic cheers. As she surfaced the second time, she searched the sea of faces for Jonathan. But Trish couldn't see him. She didn't see Paul, either.

On her third attempt to get out of the water, a couple of boys actually helped her instead of tossing her back in. Most of the crowd had dispersed by then anyway. Dripping wet and thoroughly exhausted, Trish and Mary sat on the end of the club dock trying to get their breath back.

"Why didn't you tell me about this?" Mary asked, wringing the water out of the front of her blouse. "I would have worn my bathing suit."

"I forgot. They only throw you in the first time you win," Trish replied. She gave her hair a twist and laughed. "It felt good, didn't it?"

Mary shrugged. "I wouldn't exactly use the word *good*. Besides, now I'm freezing. Let's go home."

As they boarded *Lady* to go home, Trish said, "Did you see Jonathan in that crowd?"

Mary shook her head. "I didn't really expect to see him, did you?"

"Sure. Why not?" Trish countered.

"You don't think you humiliated him? I mean, wasn't that part of your plan, part of your revenge?" Mary raised the mainsail and cleated it. It immediately started flapping ferociously in the strong wind. "Shall I shove us off?" Mary asked after she'd raised the smaller jib.

"Yes," Trish called from the stern. "Give us

a good hard shove, and I'll let the side board down."

Once they were underway, Trish said, "Actually, by beating him, I won his bet for him, didn't I? Jonathan should be glad, shouldn't he?"

Mary looked at Trish and rolled her eyes in disbelief. "It wasn't beating him so much as *how* you beat him. Your attitude was downright lousy."

"Don't you think we should have won?" Trish demanded.

"Of course we should have. We were both terrific. But Jonathan deserves some credit, too, wouldn't you say? After all, he's been coaching you. Anyway, he doesn't deserve the treatment you've been giving him the last couple of days."

"I don't know what you mean," Trish insisted, slipping one foot through the hiking strap and sliding up higher on the angled deck.

"Come off it, Trish. You know exactly what I mean. I think you owe Jonathan an apology," Mary added.

Chapter Ten

Home alone that afternoon, Trish kept wondering where Jonathan had been after the race. He almost always went to the island. Perhaps Mary was right—he was angry about Trish's attitude. Maybe the bet was something Paul had made up, or at least had exaggerated to get attention. If so, she'd played right into Paul's hands by acting the way she had toward Jonathan. Now Paul had another story to spread, this time about silly, ungrateful Trish Everett.

Trish could hear some of the sarcastic things she'd said to Jonathan replayed in her thoughts, and it wasn't so much *what* she'd said as *how* she'd said it. Jonathan had probably decided she was a jerk and wanted nothing more to do with her. If she could only undo it all, unsay everything, and start fresh. Then Jonathan could share Trish's victory with her. It *was* his victory, too. Without him, she could never have done it, and she knew it. Trish only hoped that Jonathan knew how much she appreciated him.

By dinnertime, Trish felt awful. The flush of victory was gone, leaving only the sadness of her loss. She dragged down to the dinner table when her mother called her, certain that she wouldn't be able to eat a thing.

She felt terrible when she saw that her mother had fixed her favorite dinner: cold crabmeat salad and blueberry muffins. But try as she might, Trish was unable to do more than poke at her food.

"Don't you feel good, honey?" her mother asked in a concerned voice.

"Sure she does," her father said. "She's just worn out from that race this morning. Right, Trish? I used to feel exactly the same way myself."

He gave Trish a knowing wink. "Let's just move on to dessert, Barbara. Trish can finish her salad tomorrow."

Mrs. Everett got up and disappeared into the kitchen. "Surprise!" she cried, returning to the dining room.

There, in the center of the table she set an adorable boat-shaped cake with a large glowing candle for a mast. "For she's a jolly good sailor," her parents began singing together. "For she's a jolly good sailor . . ." Trish listened to them, uncertain whether to laugh or cry.

"And that's not all, young lady," her father said when they had finished their song. "There's more to come." Trish forced herself to smile as her father produced a little hand-written scroll. "Go on," he urged. "Read it."

The scroll promised Trish the boat for the remainder of the season. Now she had everything she wanted, she told herself. Trish felt she ought to be pleased or, at least, satisfied. But she was neither.

"We're not waiting anymore to come out and watch you, either," her father told her, as he cut into the cake. "We're going to be out in the motorboat on the Fourth of July cheering you on just as we've always cheered your brother on."

"The Fourth of July!" Trish repeated with alarm.

Her mother laughed. "Thursday is the Fourth of July. Don't tell me you've forgotten your favorite summer holiday?"

But she had forgotten about it, and the extra race was only part of it. Then there was the barbecue and, finally, the fireworks. Mary would probably want to invite Deke. It was the best yacht club party of the summer, and everyone was encouraged to bring a date.

As Trish thought of Mary with Deke and herself with no one, she felt even worse. Jonathan would undoubtedly be there, but he would most likely ignore her, and Trish couldn't really blame him. He didn't have to put up with her, not anymore. Even if he did have a bet with her brother, it was over now. She'd seen to that herself.

Excusing herself, she went to her room. Trish flung herself across her bed and began to cry. Just as Mary had tried telling her, simply winning alone did not make her a winner. In fact, at the moment, Trish definitely felt as though she'd lost. She was certain she'd never get to sleep, but finally exhaustion overtook her, and she dozed off.

"Jonathan called," her mother told her when she finally came downstairs the following morning.

"What did you say to him?" Trish asked.

"I told him you were sleeping," her mother answered.

Trish felt a flood of excitement. "Did he say what he wanted?"

"No, he didn't. But he did say he'd call you back again."

"When?" Trish demanded.

"My goodness, honey." Her mother laughed.

"Well, did he say when?" Trish pressed.

"No. He simply said later."

Trish decided to call Jonathan back right away. There was so much she had to say to him. But his phone rang and rang without any answer.

Trying to busy herself around the house, Trish waited for him to call her back. When she hadn't heard from him by two o'clock, Trish could stand it no longer. She went down to the dock for a swim, but even swimming couldn't relax her.

She had told her mother to call her right away if Jonathan should call back. But, after a while, she had to go back up to the house and make sure that her mother had kept her word.

When Trish walked in the door, her mother was just about to go grocery shopping. Trish would have to wait in the house for Jonathan's call or risk missing it. After trying him one more time and getting no answer, she called Mary.

When she'd told Mary about Jonathan's call, Mary said, "You've gotten enough revenge, I take it."

"Yes!" Trish cried fervently.

"Well, if I were you, the first thing I'd do is kill my mother for not waking me up. Then I'd call Jonathan back."

Trish sighed. "I tried and he isn't home."

"Too bad," Mary sympathized.

"I'll just have to wait for him to call me back, I guess."

"It sounds that way." Mary cleared her throat and added, "While you're on the phone, can you tell me if anything special is happening on the Fourth? Isn't there a race or something?"

"There's a race at ten o'clock," Trish told her. "Then there's a barbecue with all the corn on the cob you can eat, followed by fireworks."

Mary said, "I'd like to spend the afternoon with Deke."

"You can bring Deke. He could meet us over here after the race, and we could bring him out to the island," Trish told her.

"Are you sure it's OK?" Mary asked.

"Sure. Lots of kids bring dates," Trish assured her.

"I meant with you. You know—"

"Oh, no," Trish lied. "It's fine with me. I like Deke. It'll be fun to have him there, and besides, he's probably a terrific badminton player, right? Tell him there'll be a badminton tournament on the lawn in front of the clubhouse."

"That should sell him on the barbecue, that and all the corn on the cob he can eat," Mary agreed. "I'll definitely see you Thursday morning for the race, but I'll have to double-check with Deke about the barbecue. He may have to do something at the tennis club, but I would like to show off a little for him at the yacht club. Let's leave it that he's coming, and I'll let you know if he can't."

"That's fine," Trish said, her throat closing up. Maybe she'd just let Mary and Deke go alone. They could use the motorboat to get out to the island, and she'd stay home. Maybe, at the last minute, Trish would get sick. That wouldn't be difficult, she felt sick already.

Thursday, the Fourth of July, finally arrived, and for the first time Trish could remember, she was not excited about the day. Jonathan had never called back, and after trying to call him a few more times, she had finally given up. Now Trish might never know why he had called.

"Deke's really looking forward to the barbecue," Mary told Trish when she came bounding into the Everetts' house before the race. "He said we should avoid winning today, though, so we wouldn't be wet all afternoon."

170

"They won't throw us in again," Trish assured her. "As I told you before, they only do that the *first* time you win."

"Good, because I want to win again, don't you?"

Trish shrugged.

"What's wrong?" Mary asked.

"I never got to talk to Jonathan. I kept trying to call him but never got an answer."

"How do you know he didn't try calling you? Were you here every second of every day? Maybe he tried to call you back, but no one answered here, either," Mary suggested.

"Well, whatever. The point is that I never talked with him. For all I know, he hates me."

"Oh, for heaven's sake, Trish, he doesn't hate you!"

But despite Mary's words, Trish wasn't convinced. As she dragged down to the dock with Mary, she was certain she wouldn't be able to repeat Sunday's performance. Winning, she was now convinced, took a fight, and Trish was not up to it.

"For a person who should be on top of the world, you sure seem gloomy," Mary observed as Trish lowered the boat lift.

"I've been thinking over what you said," Trish told her.

"I have, too, and I'm sorry I said any of it. Winning was the right thing to do, and you weren't all that nasty to Jonathan. I mean, calling a person by their last name in the heat of competition hardly qualifies you for witch of the year."

"I was wrong to feel so smug, so self-righteous. I was also wrong to assume that Jonathan was guilty without at least asking him about the whole thing up front. I was cowardly."

"Oh, come on. You're being too hard on yourself. Lighten up," Mary ordered. "I'll get the bucket and scrub brushes."

"What for?" Trish asked.

"To wash the bottom. We've got to wash the bottom, for heaven's sake. You don't want to lose, do you?"

"No," Trish agreed. "I guess it's too late for that."

Without saying anything more, Mary turned and walked to the shed for the bucket and brushes. After the bottom was clean, they rigged the boat and sailed out to the starting line.

Trish scanned the boats for a glimpse of Jonathan. Most of the boats were out, but Jonathan's wasn't among them. Suddenly, she imagined him sick or injured. Had she been so self-absorbed the past week that she had failed to realize that something might have happened to him? Trish began to feel even worse than she had felt before. What kind of a self-centered person was she anyway, she asked herself?

Then Trish saw Jonathan. He looked dazzling in the bright July morning, his hair nearly golden from the summer sun, his dark tan set off by a white golf shirt. Trish was still looking at Jonathan when he suddenly looked her way. Their eyes met, and he smiled. He waved and gave her a victory sign with his fingers. Trish laughed as a shiver of pure pleasure swept through her. Clearly, he was happy Trish had won. All her worrying had been for nothing. Jonathan might not be in love with her or anything, but at least he didn't hate her.

Trish couldn't take her eyes off him. There she was in all the noise and confusion of the starting line and all she could do was look at Jonathan.

"Got it!" Mary declared as the first gun was fired.

Trish snapped out of her reverie. Her training took over, and her attention turned to finding a spot on the line and figuring out what she had to do in order to have her boat in that spot when the starting gun was fired. There were twenty-four other boats around her, their crisp Dacron sails snapping loudly in the wind as they pursued their own courses. But her attention was on her own race. Jonathan had taught Trish that.

When the starting gun exploded, she was forced slightly off course by another boat who apparently had had the same idea about where to begin. But she didn't lose her concentration, and as the fleet began to thin out, *Lady* was once again among the leaders. Trish's mind was on the wind: where it was, where it was going, and how she could best use its movement to create her own.

When they reached the first buoy, Trish was again forced slightly off course. But once again, she compensated for that and stayed with the leaders.

They crossed the finish line fifth. It wasn't first, but Trish was satisfied. She had done her best, and there was always next time and the time after that. She was sure she would come in first again.

She kept sailing toward the yacht club, eager to see Jonathan. He didn't seem to hate her, and that meant Trish still had a chance with him. She knew he was out there; Trish was determined to find him.

"Where are you going?" Mary asked.

"To the island," Trish told her. "To find Jonathan."

Mary shook her head. "We've got to go back to your dock first."

"Why?" Trish demanded.

"To pick up Deke. Remember? It's the Fourth of July. You told me to invite him to the picnic at the island."

Trish groaned. She didn't want to wait another second to see Jonathan. Suppose he was out there now and left before she could get back, she asked herself.

"You told me to invite Deke," Mary reminded her.

"Oh, Mary, I'm sorry. It isn't what you think at all. I was just eager to get out to the island and see Jonathan. He smiled at me today, and I know now that he's not mad at me. I wanted to see him before he got away." Trish came about and headed *Lady* toward the Everetts' house.

"So, not only are you finished with your revenge, you aren't even mad at Jonathan anymore, are you?" Mary asked.

"How could I be? I'm just glad he's not mad at me. I decided Paul could have exaggerated the story to impress whomever he was talking to. There might have been some truth to what he said, but Clark's bet couldn't be the only reason Jonathan helped me."

"But what if it was? What if Paul was telling the unexaggerated truth?" Mary pressed.

Trish hesitated. Then she said firmly, "It doesn't matter anymore. I don't even want to know."

"There's Deke!" Mary cried excitedly as they neared the Everetts' dock. "But wait a minute. He isn't alone."

Trish looked at the second figure standing next to Deke. "It's probably my dad," she said.

"Are your mom and dad going to the yacht club picnic?"

"They'll probably come out later for the fireworks," Trish answered.

"How will they get to the island if we take your motorboat?"

"They always—" Trish began, but Mary cut her off.

"Say! That's not your dad! That's—"

"Jonathan!" Trish finished for her.

Both boys were waving as the girls sailed up.

"Jonathan!" Trish cried, scrambling off the boat. "How did you get here?"

Jonathan laughed, his emerald eyes twinkling. "I had a good-size lead. After I finished the race, I sailed right home and got the car. I was hoping you'd take a drive with me before the barbecue. I didn't think Deke would be here."

"Don't mind us," Mary told him. "We can wait up at the house or something until you get back from your drive."

"Better yet, Mary and I can go on out to the party and meet you two there later," Deke said.

"Good idea. You know how to run the motorboat, don't you, Mary?" Trish asked.

Mary shook her head. "I might be able to figure it out, though."

"I can run a motorboat. No problem," Deke assured her.

"It's settled, then," Jonathan said. "We'll meet you two later. We can take my car back to my house and take the cruiser out to the island."

"Goodbye, then," Mary said, and Deke waved as he helped her into the boat.

When Trish and Jonathan reached the Everetts' front yard, Jonathan said, "Where to?"

"Anywhere is fine with me," she replied.

He shook his head. "I'm afraid anywhere won't do. How about Al's on the Lake?"

"Now?" Trish asked, astounded. She hadn't even had time to brush her hair after the race. She had to look totally disheveled.

"Why not? It's almost one o'clock."

"But what about the barbecue? What about Mary and Deke?" Trish demanded.

Jonathan laughed. "Mary and Deke can get along without us for a while. We'll go out there later—after we've talked."

"But my hair!" she protested.

"You look fine. Remember, most people get to Al's by boat, especially during the day on a

176

holiday." He gently brushed the hair back from her cheek. "I like your hair just the way it is."

She wanted to thank him for the compliment and then return it by telling him how she liked his hair, so thick and sun streaked. But she couldn't because she was too embarrassed. "At least I'm not all wet," she said instead, thinking of the first time Jonathan had seen her.

"I'm sorry I wasn't there Sunday to see that you got a proper dunking," Jonathan said, obviously thinking Trish was referring to that when she mentioned having wet hair. "Paul had to get right home, and I had no choice but to take him as I'd promised."

"Then you weren't angry with me?" she asked.

"Angry?" He sounded flabbergasted. "Why would I be angry with you? You're the best student I've ever had, not to mention the prettiest."

As she watched him walk around the car to the driver's side, she felt herself blush—more with amazement than with embarrassment. If there had been a bet, she'd won it for him. Jonathan didn't need to be nice to her just to keep her interested in taking lessons from him. After all, weren't the lessons over?

He must really care for her, Trish told herself. Had he come over that day to finally tell her that? Part of her wanted to simply wait and see, but a larger part of her demanded that she ask outright to avoid another unfulfilling scene similar to the one they'd had on the dock after they'd gone out for pizza.

After he was in the car, Trish made herself say, "What are we going to talk about?"

"Don't you know?" He turned, focusing all the intensity of his green eyes on her.

"Yes," she said. "I guess I do know something *I* want to talk about."

He started up the engine and began backing out of the driveway. "OK," he said. "Shoot."

Was she crazy, she asked herself? Here he was taking her out to lunch at Al's, the fanciest restaurant on Sand Lake. He had just told her she was pretty. He was going to spend the entire afternoon and evening with her on a double date with her best friend, something she and Mary had been dreaming of since the first time they'd seen him at the end of May. All that, and she was about to ruin everything by mentioning the stupid bet. Earlier, Trish had decided to forget all about it, but she knew now she couldn't ever forget it unless she got it out in the open. Whatever the risk, Trish had to know just how big a role that bet played in Jonathan's feelings for her.

Trish began by saying, "I didn't exactly get this information firsthand. I sort of overheard a conversation. I didn't mean to eavesdrop, but—"

"Let me guess," Jonathan interrupted. "You heard Paul talking about the bet I made with your brother when you came out to the island for a lesson that day you ran off."

"How did you know?"

"I didn't. But I guessed. At first I thought I should never have told Paul about the bet. I probably wouldn't have told him, either, if I thought it was all that important. He can be a real creep sometimes. But then, believe it or not, he also can be a darn good friend. In fact, he was the one that told me he thought you might have overheard him talking to Stew Harris, and he didn't have to do that. Paul knew I'd be angry, but he told me anyway because he felt bad about it."

Jonathan paused for a moment to adjust his rearview mirror, then he went on. "At first I thought I would just deny the whole thing, but I couldn't do that to you. I felt you deserved more than a lie, so I called you to talk. But you were so angry I couldn't bring myself to say anything, not over the phone."

Jonathan pulled the car into Al's parking lot and parked. "So," he went on, shutting off the engine, "when you suggested getting together before my class the other day, I thought that would be the perfect opportunity to tell you how sorry I was, not about the bet really, but about the way you had to learn about it. Then you brought Mary with you, and I couldn't say what I'd planned to say in front of her."

Jonathan's hand brushed Trish's as he rested it on the seat between them. When she didn't take her hand away, he covered her hand with his.

"I was afraid that your anger would undo all the progress you'd made," he went on, stroking the backs of her fingers. "Then you won the race!" Jonathan shook his head. "You're a truly remarkable girl."

Trish decided it was time for her both to forgive him and to thank him. Whatever was going to happen between them in the future, he had been an integral part of bringing her to where she was in the present. Looking at the dashboard, she said, "I owe you a lot, Jonathan. Without your help I would have continued to come in last until Clark came home and reclaimed the boat. You got me on the right track whatever your reasons." But thanking him was even harder than forgiving him.

Suddenly, there didn't seem to be any air in the car. She reached for the car door.

"Don't you want to hear what the bet was?" he asked, taking hold of her arm to stop her from getting out of the car.

"I know all I need to know, all I *want* to know," she told him. She just wanted to move on now, to forget the past and enjoy the present. Jonathan let go of her arm, allowing her to open her own door. Trish got out of the car.

"So, let's go in and eat. I mean it," she said, poking her head back through the open car door. "Suddenly I'm famished."

"Too bad the doughnuts I brought to the strategy session wouldn't keep," he said, getting out and coming around the car. When he reached her, he closed her door and took her hand in his.

"Doughnuts! So it was doughnuts you brought me, after all. I thought maybe you'd brought me flowers." She laughed.

Jonathan laughed. "I did. I brought you roses

from my mother's garden last Friday. They were going to be part of the apology Mary's presence discouraged me from making." They started toward the door to the restaurant.

"I suppose they didn't keep any better than the doughnuts," she teased.

"There are more roses where those came from," Jonathan assured her, opening the door and ushering her in. Immediately Trish saw that the restaurant was packed.

"Maybe we should skip lunch and head on out to the island," she suggested.

Jonathan asked, "Why?"

"It's awfully crowded," Trish answered. "It's going to take quite awhile just to get a table."

"I've got a reservation," Jonathan told her with that mischievous grin of his.

Trish gave him a sideways glance. "You're awfully sure of yourself, aren't you?"

He nodded. "When I couldn't get you on the phone earlier in the week, I decided I'd just have to overwhelm you with my dramatic presence."

"And did you?" Trish laughed, deciding not to tell him how many times she'd tried calling him back—at least not right then.

"You tell me," Jonathan countered.

"You did," Trish answered truthfully.

"Two for Stewart," he told the head waiter.

The head waiter led them to a table for two on the patio, overlooking the lake. "Good grief!" Trish couldn't help exclaiming when she looked at the menu. "These are awfully high prices for lunch, aren't they?"

Jonathan smiled. "Ah, you're forgetting. You won that bet I had with your brother for me on Sunday. This lunch is on Clark."

"In that case, I'll have the lobster salad," she told him.

"We really ought to thank your brother, you know," Jonathan told her, looking suddenly serious.

"Really? For what?" she asked as their hands found each other across the table.

"For bringing us together. I thought you were cute the first time I saw you, but it took the lessons and all to make me realize just how I felt about you," he confessed.

"So, why have you waited so long to tell me?" Trish demanded.

Jonathan gave her hand a squeeze. "I didn't want our relationship to interfere with your sailing progress."

She pulled her hand away. "Because of the bet, no doubt."

"No, not because of the bet. The bet was Clark's idea, not mine. No, I saw you were good, very good. I saw that you could be one of the best. And look"—he smiled triumphantly—"you are."

He leaned across the table then and gave her a short kiss on the lips. As he drew back, his eyes held hers and her mouth burned for more.

"I wish we were alone," she said softly, her gaze dropping to the tablecloth.

"We will be," he assured her.

Trish looked into his smoldering green eyes.

Jonathan looked so confident that it suddenly gave her an uneasy feeling.

"Don't expect me to let you win," Trish told him forcefully, just to set him straight.

Jonathan laughed. "Don't expect *me* to let you win, either. I haven't yet. And I don't intend to start. You'll have to work for your victories. But, when we're not racing—"

She put a finger to his lips to silence him. "I know," Trish said as the waiter arrived to take their order.

And she did, too. She also knew that the best part of this now-wonderful summer was yet to come. Trish knew what winning was all about because she finally felt as though she were a winner. The Fourth of July sun was still blazing, but the fireworks had definitely begun.

ALL THAT GLITTERS

It's the New Hit Series from Bantam Books that takes you behind the scenes of a T.V. Soap Opera.

Share the highs and lows, the hits and flops, the glamour and hard work, the glory and heartache of life on the
Soap Set with:

KATIE	SHANA	MITCH
NOLAN	**BRADBURY**	**CALLAHAN**

Each a star in their own right, each a seasoned professional aiming for the top, each a teenager dealing with the ups and downs, the crazy ins and outs of teenage life—all in the glaring light of the camera's all-seeing eye!

ALL THAT GLITTERS
It's Golden!

Janet Quin-Harkin's Sugar & Spice

Watch out for a smashing new series from the best-selling author, Janet Quin-Harkin.

Meet the most unlikely pair of best friends since Toni and Jill from Janet Quin-Harkin's TEN BOY SUMMER.

Caroline's thrilled to find out she's got a long-lost cousin exactly her age. But she's horrified when Chrissy comes to spend a year with her family. Caroline's a reserved and polite only child – now she has to share her life with a loud, unsophisticated, embarrassing farm girl!

Coming soon – wherever Bantam paperbacks are sold!